## Hayley's dog, Mack, began to emit a steady, high whine...

His head was up, nose pricked. Hayley's gut clenched. Were their pursuers within scenting distance already? She increased their speed as greatly as she dared. Behind her, Sean's breathing was coming in deep puffs.

"Not much longer," she said.

Suddenly, a large animal heaved to its feet from among the bushes lining the river. The moose let out a moaning cry and turned tail, its shaggy coat becoming flashes of black amongst the trees.

Behind Hayley, Mack's whine changed to a full-throated bark. She swiveled to witness her dog lunge from Sean's arms into hot pursuit. The lunge sent the ATF agent sprawling backward into the creek with a great splash.

Hayley's heart plummeted to her toes. Their situation had gone from deep distress to the verge of disaster. Unless they stopped to build a fire and dry Sean's clothing, hypothermia would quickly claim his life. But if they stopped, bullets would soon end both their lives...

**Jill Elizabeth Nelson** writes what she likes to read—faith-based tales of adventure seasoned with romance. Parts of the year find her and her husband on the international mission field. Other parts find them at home in rural Minnesota, surrounded by the woods and prairie and their four grown children and young grandchildren. More about Jill and her books can be found at jillelizabethnelson.com or Facebook.com/jillelizabethnelson.author.

### Books by Jill Elizabeth Nelson

### Love Inspired Suspense

Visit the Author Profile page at LoveInspired.com.

# HUNTED
# IN ALASKA

## JILL ELIZABETH NELSON

**LOVE INSPIRED** SUSPENSE

INSPIRATIONAL ROMANCE

# LOVE INSPIRED® SUSPENSE
### INSPIRATIONAL ROMANCE

Recycling programs for this product may not exist in your area.

ISBN-13: 978-1-335-58813-5

Hunted in Alaska

Love Inspired
22 Adelaide St. West, 41st Floor
Toronto, Ontario M5H 4E3, Canada
www.LoveInspired.com

**Printed in U.S.A.**

Many there be which say of my soul,
There is no help for him in God. Selah.
But thou, O Lord, art a shield for me; my glory,
and the lifter up of mine head.
—*Psalm* 3:2-3

To all who choose to trust in the Lord
despite pain, loss, difficulties or danger. God is faithful.

# ONE

The sharp tang of wood stain teased Hayley Brent's nostrils as she dipped her two-inch-wide brush into a can of thick sable-brown liquid. Deftly, she removed excess stain against the lip of the can, then brought the brush to the work in progress. The tip of her tongue caught between her teeth—a mannerism her brother, Craig, often teased her about—she pressed the wet bristles into a deep groove in the wood and smoothly swiped the stain from one end of the groove to the other. Taking a step back, she scanned the entire carving up and down. Her heart rate kicked up a little faster. This piece was her magnum opus thus far in her career. Could she hope it would be her breakthrough?

The immense and graphically detailed chain saw carving of an eagle clutching a salmon in its talons loomed four feet taller than her five-foot-eight-inch height. Last week, just before Craig left for Seattle to do research for a writing assignment, Hayley had finished the carving process with the chain saw. From then until yesterday she'd labored on the detail work with a chisel and sandpaper. Now she was in the homestretch with stain and sealant. A lot of sweat and effort was invested in this commissioned piece for a deep-pocketed and influential customer in the Lower 48. If this guy was enthused with the carving, her name as a chain saw artist would be made. She could count on shipping many more pieces south to the contiguous United States from her home in the Alaskan interior. A dream realized.

As Hayley reached her brush toward the can of stain, a deep-throated bark shattered her concentration and she gave a little jump. Frowning, she laid the brush flat across the stain can's open top and went to the screen door of the cavernous, well-ventilated shed where she did her work. As always, her breath caught at the wild beauty of the Alaskan wilderness.

To her left, a boreal forest of white-barked birch trees and stately black spruce framed the sturdy, compact cabin she and her brother considered home base from late spring through mid-fall. Straight ahead, splashes of blue and gold vied with vivid greens in the myriad jumble of plants and shrubs that ushered the eye toward a small, sparkling aqua lake. There, her dock led to the yellow Piper Cub floatplane that was the only transportation in or out of her remote location. Now, at the end of September, nature was putting on its last great show before snow and ice swept in and dominated for at least the next six months. By then, she would be in Fairbanks for the winter, but for now, she meant to finish her vital project and enjoy the peace and solitude.

A rumbling growl drew her gaze to the right. Her deep-chested Alaskan malamute stood stiff and still in the meadow. The breed-distinctive plume of his tail curved across his broad sable back, hairs bristling. His triangle-shaped ears stood pricked to attention. Something wasn't right.

Hayley's gut clenched. "What is it, Mack?"

The dog darted a glance at her with almond-shaped brown eyes, then returned his attention to the pristine blue sky above them. Not some critter in the woods, then. Was somebody flying in? She wasn't expecting anyone.

Hayley stepped out the door, her sturdy

work boots crunching on the gravel lining the edges of the work shed. Denim jeans and a long-sleeved shirt beneath a padded vest covered most of her lean frame, but the fall breeze brushed chilly fingers across the exposed skin of her hands and face. A strand of tawny hair escaped her ponytail and swept across her mouth. She tugged the hair away as she gazed upward, straining her ears for plane engine noise. There it was. Faint, but growing louder in the south. Might be someone passing over, but the engine rumble sounded low to the ground as if the plane might be coming in for a landing.

Suddenly, a red-and-white aircraft broke into view over the tops of the trees, sparking an explosion of throaty barks from Mack. The unfamiliar plane dwarfed her Cub. This long, big-bellied type of aircraft would be capable of transporting the carved eagle, but no such arrangements had yet been made. Hayley's gaze riveted on the tail of the plane. No identifying numbers or letters. Lack of a call sign often meant one of two things—poachers or smugglers. Dangerous people. Hayley's gut clenched.

With one hand, she shaded her eyes from the westering sun and stared up into the cockpit. The plane skimmed low enough that she made out the figures of two men. The one seated in the copilot position seemed to get agitated at the sight of her. As the man gestured toward the pilot and then pointed at her, he waved a bulky black item in the air: an automatic assault rifle.

Ice congealed in Hayley's lungs. Nearly everyone in the state of Alaska owned guns, but full automatics weren't the norm. Those were mostly in the hands of the military, law enforcement or crooks. These guys weren't soldiers or cops, and they were not happy to see her.

In seconds, the plane shot beyond her property and continued toward a wall of forest half a mile away. Evidently, the pilot had never intended to land his craft in *her* lake, but he clearly meant to land somewhere close at hand. The nearest body of water to hers was a slightly larger lake about a mile away, where a warehouse-like building sat moldering on the bank. The structure used to serve as a way station for a regional dogsled race, but when the route had been redrawn a decade ago, the building was abandoned. There was no good reason for anyone to land a plane there. Hayley's jaw clenched. *No good* summed up what these guys were all about.

She took off for her cabin with Mack loping at her heels. Would her presence be a deterrent to their agenda? Hopefully so. Or would they come after her? Surely not.

Poachers and smugglers preferred to keep a low profile, not draw attention to themselves by attacking people. Then again, they didn't like leaving witnesses to their activities. No matter what, she needed to alert the authorities about an unmarked plane landing in a location where there couldn't possibly be a legitimate purpose. Then she needed to grab the engine key for the Cub and get out of here while law enforcement did their job.

Clomping across the cabin's generous porch, she reached the door and pushed inside. Warmth with a hint of cedar scent greeted her as she strode to the bulky wooden desk on the far left side of the living room space and picked up her satellite phone, a necessity in these environs where cellular service was spotty to nonexistent.

Hayley punched in the emergency numbers and waited and waited and…nothing. She glared at the phone. The handset was turned on, but it wasn't connecting to a satellite. That never happened. What was going on?

Airplane engine buzz grew louder outside.

Hayley's heartbeat stalled, then ratcheted into overdrive. The armed intruders were returning. She darted to the picture window and peered out. The large floatplane was nearing touchdown on her lake, meaning the route to her Cub was cut off. What should she do?

Hope for the best; prepare for the worst—one of her brother's cliché sayings that often drew an eye roll from her, but today sounded like sage advice. Heart thumping, she turned toward Mack. The dog eyed her with focused intensity, waiting for her word.

"We may have to bust out the back door and run for the woods," she told him. "Let's get ready to move."

Mack answered with a solemn *woof* as if he understood everything she said.

Hayley hustled to the closet and pulled out her hiking backpack. Wilderness Alaskans kept an emergency pack filled and ready. She set the bulging pack on the floor behind the sofa and quickly stuffed the satellite phone into a side pocket. Then she returned to the closet, grabbed her down-filled parka and tossed it on top of the pack. The temperature dropped dramatically after dark, and who knew how long she might have to hide. A hiking pack and a jacket—little enough preparation for the worst, but she was out of time.

Outside, the plane's engine was already ratcheting down. Whoever these people were, they had landed on her property carrying assault weapons Hayley's pulse hammered in her throat as she pulled her bolt-action Winchester Model 70 Featherweight rifle off the gun rack and loaded it with .30-06 cartridges.

*Please, God, help. I don't want to have to shoot anyone.* She was proficient in handling the rifle, and a more than adequate shot, but she'd never fired at a person before. Could she bring herself to do it?

"Hello, the house," a pleasant baritone voice called from outside. "Permission to approach."

Holding her breath, Hayley peered out the window. From the plane's cockpit, two people gazed out toward her cabin, but neither was the person trying to communicate. The craft's passenger door stood open, and a tall, dark-haired man was stepping off the dock into her meadow. The man was too far away for her to make out his features, except that he had a close-cropped beard and a muscular build. He was dressed in black jeans and a dark brown jacket. An ebony strap around his shoulder indicated the presence of a firearm at his back, but both of his hands were empty and raised to shoulder height, palms out.

Tension eased in Hayley's gut. Could she have overreacted? Maybe these guys were no threat. Her jaw firmed. No, a lone woman in the Alaskan wilderness couldn't possibly overreact to armed strangers trespassing on her property.

Hayley pulled her front door ajar but didn't step outside. Instead, she sheltered behind the thick wooden panel. Growling, Mack moved forward, but she grabbed his collar and held him back. The dog went still, though his coarse fur bristled against her fingers.

"I'm armed," she called out. "I have a dog, and I've been on the satellite phone." No need to tell them she hadn't gotten through to anyone.

"All of that is understandable," the reasonable-voiced man answered. "Let me come on up and—"

A masculine yell brimming with profanity interrupted the man's words. Hayley peeked around the edge of the door. Breath fled her lungs as her pulse jackhammered in her ears. One…two…three…no—four men leaped out of the red-and-white plane onto her dock and charged toward the cabin, weapons trained.

The man who'd been talking to her whirled on his buddies, reaching toward them and hollering as if trying to stop their rush. But the foursome barreled past the dark-haired spokesman, nearly knocking him off his feet. Their automatic weapons erupted in a stream of bullets.

The cabin's picture window exploded inward. Glass shards stung Hayley's torso, and particularly her exposed hands and face. The rifle fell from her grip. She threw herself to the floor, hauling Mack down with her. Whatever she did now had to happen fast. These guys meant to kill her.

Heart in his throat, Sean O'Keefe grabbed for Wade Becker as the hothead and his cronies swept past him, blasting their guns in full-automatic mode. He missed the grab and staggered, nearly hitting the ground.

When the boss man had ordered their plane to turn around and land here so they could *deal with the problem*, Sean had talked fast. He thought he'd convinced him and the rest of the gang that it would be wise to go easy on the unexpected innocent witness to their rendezvous with the buyer. Subduing the woman and tying her up until they were gone should have been sufficient, especially when the crew planned to disband and disappear after this crucial deal. Why add murder to their rap sheets? But, as usual, Becker couldn't contain his violent impulses, and this time a civilian was paying the price.

What could possibly be a worse ending to Sean's undercover assignment with the federal Bureau of Alcohol, Tobacco, Firearms and Explosives? He grimaced. The thing he needed to do next might make that cut. He was probably too late, but he had to stop the attack even if he blew his cover or got himself killed.

Sean shrugged his M16 rifle from his shoulder into his hands and swept a burst of bullets toward the heels of the lowlifes he'd been forced to rub shoulders with for the past five months. The foursome jumped and ceased fire. Whirling, they pointed their weapons at Sean's chest.

Becker called him a foul name. "What do you think you're doing?"

Sean met the man's molten stare. "I'm not adding murder to my rap sheet just because you guys like to shoot first and think later. Assaulting the cabin was never the plan."

"Plans change," said a flinty voice behind him.

Sean looked over his shoulder to find Sherman Patterson standing on the dock. The man's empty, inky stare reminded Sean of a python he'd once seen eyeing a rodent in a zoo. As far as character quality went, Sean would rate the reptile over Patterson any day. Even out here in the Alaskan wilderness, the guy wore an impeccably cut three-piece suit and designer loafers and every salt-and-pepper strand of thick and glossy hair was locked in place. A snake in a suit, and from day one of his undercover assignment, Sean had been looking forward to slapping the cuffs on him. But if the woman in the house was still alive, to get her out of here he might have to kiss that dream goodbye.

Sean schooled his expression to reflect indifference. "I'll go up there and see if these trigger-happies—" he jerked his chin toward Becker and his bunch "—accomplished anything."

The quartet of shooters scowled at him, but Patterson nodded. "Be my guest. Let us know if you run into her gun or her dog." A thin smile flickered across the man's sharp features.

Gut roiling, Sean trotted toward the silent cabin. Every hair on his body stood on end. If she was alive in there, he could take a bullet from her at any moment. But if she hadn't returned fire by now, she was probably incapable of it. These thugs he'd been running with over the past excruciating months knew that fact as well as he did. He glanced at them over his shoulder. Becker's quartet wore smug sneers on their faces. Patterson had retreated into the plane. Typical. Never one to risk his neck or get his hands dirty.

Sean reached the cabin and soft-footed up two stairs and across the porch boards. The front door hung open, peppered with bullet holes. Swallowing hard, he stepped over the threshold and peered into a living area. A hunting rifle lay at the foot of a shredded sofa, explaining why he hadn't been shot while approaching the cabin.

His gaze searched the space. No one in view, neither dog nor human, but a few droplets of red speckled the floor. Sean drew in a stuttering breath. Clearly, someone in here was wounded, though they'd been able to move. Did he dare hope the woman and her pooch had escaped through the kitchen and out the back door? He scanned the kitchen area that formed an L with the living room. Shattered crockery covered the space, and the back door sported multiple bullet holes.

Not likely she would have survived attempting that exit.

No blood speckles led in that direction. They did, however, lead toward the far wall of the living space. There, a closed door adjoined a set of rustic wooden stairs that gave access to the second story. Had she retreated up there?

"Ma'am," Sean called out. "I know you have no reason to trust me, but I've come to help."

Even as he spoke, rustles and thumps drew him toward the closed door. A few bullet holes marked the wood, but not as many as on the back and front doors. With debris crunching under his work boots, Sean moved in that direction. As he stepped beyond the sofa, his gaze passed over a bulging backpack and a heavy parka. She'd prepared to retreat, but Becker's sudden aggression had thwarted her plan.

Sean reached the door and gripped the knob. It wouldn't turn. The effort was greeted by a dog's whine followed by a few hushed, unintelligible words. His heart jumped. The woman was alive—the dog, too. He needed to get beyond that locked door and usher them out of the cabin to take cover in the woods, and he needed to do it fast. Becker's bunch could run out of their minuscule stock of patience and charge up here at any moment. He couldn't take time to coax her into letting him inside. If that were even possible.

Sean drew back his leg and rammed his heel into the door on a sweet spot beside the knob. The locking mechanism gave way, and the door panel crashed open. The dog's hindquarters were just disappearing through a small, square window in the far wall of the bathroom. The woman whirled from helping her dog get through the tight space and let out a hoarse gasp. Liquid brown eyes as wide as dinner plates stared at him. She pressed her back against the far wall, chin up, as if facing a firing squad with all the courage she could muster.

Light brown hair framed an oval face marked with several trickles of red. No doubt she'd been hit by glass shards from the shattered picture window. Her raised hands, too, showed blood smears. Sean's gaze flicked around the room. Signs of blood in the enormous, claw-foot bathtub. Smart woman. If she and her dog hadn't taken cover there, they probably wouldn't have survived the barrage the cabin had absorbed.

"You need to go." He made his tone low but urgent.

"Go?" She blinked at him as if his words had been gibberish.

"Now!" His semi-snarl brought a rush of color to her face, cutting through the shock and confusion.

She turned toward the open window and began to hoist herself over the sill.

"Not that way," Sean said. "Grab your pack and your jacket and scoot out the back door. I'll cover for you. Move fast."

The woman swiveled toward him with a tentative nod. Sean stepped back to allow her to leave the bathroom. Shoulders hunched, she rushed past him. She snatched the jacket and shrugged it on but didn't take time to zip it. Then she threw the pack over her shoulders and headed toward the back door.

Moving smoothly and quickly, Sean hefted her rifle and followed her into the kitchen. "Wait. You might need this out there."

The woman paused and turned. He held the weapon toward her.

She reached toward the rifle, then froze, meeting his gaze. "Why are you helping me?"

"No time to explain."

Jerking a nod, she grabbed the rifle even as booted feet sounded on the porch boards.

"What's going on in there?" Becker's nasally voice called. "Did we get her?"

Sean whirled toward the sound. The hothead's shadow fell across the threshold. Without hesitation, Sean pressed the trigger on his M16. Bullets chattered into the floorboards, hopefully driving the assailant backward. A high-pitched yelp came from outside the door, and boots hammered the porch in hasty retreat.

A chill gripped Sean's core. He was now these weapons smugglers' declared enemy, not a pretend ally. He'd hoped to get the woman away before any of them investigated. Then he could say he'd found the cabin empty and do his best to keep them from going after her by convincing them she posed no threat wandering around in the wilderness. Considering how these guys had already proven their deadly intent, that strategy had always been a slim hope. Still, it had been worth a shot at keeping enough trust with these lowlifes until he finished his assignment. Not happening.

Sean turned on his heel and charged after the woman who was bounding out the back door. His long stride overtook her, and with a hand on her back, he pushed her into faster gear across the grass toward the tree line about ten yards distant. A large malamute raced up to them, then turned and ran alongside the woman. Behind them, multiple automatic weapons opened fire in a cacophony of lead. A bullet's slipstream kissed his cheek as a high whine nipped his eardrum.

So far, their adversaries were shooting through windows and doors on the far side of the cabin, but soon they'd either come around the structure or barrel straight through it to gain an unobstructed view of their targets. Sean took a firm grip on the woman's elbow and pulled her out of line with the back door and the kitchen window. The move temporarily put more of the bulk of the cabin between their bodies and the bullets chasing them.

A few more strides and the forest swallowed them. But Sean didn't count them safe yet. These guys would come after them, and they would have no mercy.

# TWO

Legs pumping, Hayley's heart flailed against her ribs and her lungs labored. Every molecule in her body tingled as all five senses sucked in data like a supercomputer. The thwap of bullets against tree trunks. The sharp scent of evergreen and the faintly sour odor of damp forest mulch that squished beneath her booted feet. The weight of her pack against her shoulders. The stranger's pounding footsteps behind her. Mack's panting as he loped beside her. Adrenaline's bitter, metallic taste on her tongue.

The chugging of automatic gunfire abruptly ceased, giving way to furious shouts that grew fainter behind them with every stride. Her footsteps slowed, but the man beside her pressed a hand against her shoulder.

"Keep running," he growled. "We need as much distance as we can get."

Hayley increased her pace, but only because he spoke sense, not because she trusted this guy. Who was he? Why had he risked his life for her by going against his crooked buddies? Maybe he didn't have a taste for murder, but that didn't mean he wasn't a criminal. Still, he *had* helped her.

"Follow me," she panted out. "I know these woods."

Hayley dug deep and found a new speed that sent her bounding along a barely discernible wildlife trail that twisted and turned between trunks of spruce, birch and aspen. Sweat coated her body. Yet, as the sun sank beneath the horizon and dusk overtook the land, the fall breeze nipped her skin. Full night would be upon them quickly. They would need shelter from the temperatures that would soon dip near freezing, as well as from four-footed predators that roamed the wilderness at night.

Would the human predators they'd left behind at her cabin be able to hunt in the dark? She didn't know the answer to that question, but maybe the guy running at her heels might be able to tell her. A mile, maybe even two, over uneven terrain and across small rivulets passed beneath their feet.

"Let's dial the pace back a little now." The stranger huffed out the words.

Hayley slowed but kept the lead. The nape of her neck prickled. The man who trotted at her heels carried a dangerous weapon. Thus far, he hadn't seemed inclined to use it against her, but would that situation continue?

She came to a halt and turned on the man, taking in her first solid assessment of his appearance. The light was nearly gone, but she could make out a few details. Not much older than herself, probably late twenties or early thirties. He stood several inches taller than her. Maybe around six feet in height. His build was lean but solid. A close-cropped black beard, neatly trimmed mustache and thick black hair framed a square face with a prominent nose, dark eyebrows and coffee-colored eyes. The cut of his features suggested the possibility of indigenous blood in his background. Not unusual in Alaska. Overall, a strikingly attractive man. But good looks could easily mask bad intentions.

Hayley lifted her rifle but didn't point it at him. Not yet.

"We need to talk," she said. Too bad her words wheezed between her teeth, not sounding at all tough.

"I agree, but not in the middle of the trail. You said you know these woods. Is there anywhere we can go to shelter for the night? It's unlikely we'll be pursued into the woods in the dark, so we should be okay until—"

"Morning, when they come after us." Hayley finished the man's sentence.

He jerked a nod.

She exhaled a long breath. "There's a small cave near here, but the climb to it is a little steep."

"No problem. Will your dog be able to make it?"

Hayley looked down at Mack, who panted beside her, tongue lolling. "We'll have to help him. I'm not leaving him on his own in the forest. Too many bears and wolves out here."

"Agreed." The man held out his hand toward Mack.

The dog sniffed it, then wagged his tail.

Hayley scowled. This guy might be making headway with her dog, but she wasn't anywhere near ready to count him trustworthy. Then again, she couldn't write him off as an enemy either. Of all things in life designed to aggravate her, confusion and ambiguity topped the list. She'd get to the bottom of this guy if it was the last thing she did. She could only hope it *wasn't* the last thing she did.

Whirling on her heel, Hayley continued to lead the way at a fast walk. She positioned herself slightly to one side on the trail so she could keep an eye on the guy's behavior through her peripheral vision. He moved in her wake with confident steps, but no hint of menace. His head was on a swivel as he kept scanning their environment. In a situation like this, she could appreciate his awareness level.

The terrain began to rise, and soon progress became like ascending a steep staircase. Hayley's breath labored, and a soft huff came from the stranger with every onward and upward stride. The mulch of forest detritus underfoot gradually changed to rocky scree that crunched beneath their boots. Then, through the gloom, a misty-gray wall confronted them. Not a sheer rock face by any means, but steep enough to require hands and feet to climb. The rock was pocked and slashed by indentations and crevices offering foot and handholds.

Hayley shrugged out of her pack but kept a firm grip on her rifle. She let the pack fall to the ground with a soft thump. Her breathing was slightly ragged from the upward trek, and her hands and face stung in the spots where she'd had unfriendly encounters with flying glass. She ignored the discomfort. Her wounds could be so much worse, and the time to deal with them was not yet.

"I've got some rope in here," she told the stranger as she unzipped her pack. "I'm going to leave both ends with you and climb up to the cave holding a middle portion between my teeth. I need you to tie one end of the rope around Mack's chest just behind his front legs and the other around his belly in front of his hind legs. Then you can climb up and join me. It's not far, only about six yards to the ledge, but I'll need your help to—"

"Pull him up to the cave," he said.

"Right," Hayley confirmed with a scowl. Finishing each other's sentences could get to be a bad habit, but at least he'd caught on quickly to the plan.

She pulled the rope from her pack, set the coiled line on the rocky ground, then started to sling the pack onto her shoulders again. The stranger grabbed a strap and stopped her. Heart hammering, she yanked it from his grip and backed away from him.

He lifted his hands in a placating gesture.

"You should let me bear the burden up the cliff."

"Don't be delusional." Hayley glared at him. "You've got a lot of explaining to do before I'll leave my supplies in your hands."

"Fair enough. I'll be here to catch you if the weight drags you backward and you fall."

Hayley let out a wordless growl at his faintly amused tone. This guy was *probably* a crook, but he was *definitely* a smart aleck. She centered the pack on her back, and then made sure her rifle strap was situated securely around her shoulder. If Mr. Smug thought a little extra weight was going to bring her down from the cliff, he could just watch and learn better.

Since her hands were going to be occupied with the climb, she'd need to carry the rope for her dog by another method. She found the ends of the rope, left them on the ground, then clamped her jaws around a central portion of the sturdy cord. Reaching upward, she located handholds and began to ascend the rock wall.

Sharp pains stabbed the backs of her hands and warm blood trickled from the injuries. Tears stung her eyes. Glass must be embedded in a few of the wounds. Thankfully, her palms and fingers were unaffected, allowing her to maintain a sure grip. Her shoulder muscles screamed from the weight of the pack compounded by the weight of her body as she pulled herself toward the lip of the ledge where the cave punctured the face of the cliff.

Blowing hard through her nostrils, Hayley finally reached the outcropping and collapsed onto it. She plucked the rope from between her teeth and sucked in open-mouthed drafts of pure, sweet oxygen.

"Are you okay up there?"

The man's urgent call snapped Hayley's attention back to the business at hand. Ignoring her body's protests, she hauled herself to her feet. With a groan, she shrugged out of the heavy pack and set it at the edge of the cave mouth behind her.

"I'm fine," she panted out. "Are you ready down there?"

"The ropes are secured, and I'm on my way," the man said.

His dark figure was only a shadow against the milky cliff face as he made his way toward her. Soon, he joined her on the ledge. High whines from Mack drifted up from below.

"He doesn't like being left behind," Hayley murmured to the stranger.

"No one does," he answered. "Let's help him join us."

Biting back outcries from sharp pains in her hands, Hayley joined the man in pulling Mack upward. The dog's whines intensified, but he didn't struggle.

"Good boy," Hayley called to him. "Hang in there. We've got you."

Nearing the ledge, the malamute gathered himself and lunged toward the safety of the solid ground. The line jerked through Hayley's grip, burning her palms. Mack's hindquarters dropped. Hayley yelped and renewed her grip on the rope. The stranger leaned his weight against the cord, yanking upward. Mack scrambled onto the ledge in a flurry of fur and scraping claws.

At the sudden release of the rope's tension, Hayley landed hard on her backside. The jar rattled her teeth. Mack rushed her and mashed her flat with his sturdy body. The contours of her rifle dug into her back while his rough, warm tongue slobbered her face. She let out a sob and buried her hands in his fur.

A beam of light suddenly illuminated her, and Hayley blinked up at the stranger standing over her and her dog. He'd activated the flashlight app on his phone. Her mouth went dry as she stared up at the looming shadow behind the light. What did this man plan to do now? On the ground, with her rifle beneath her, she was at his mercy.

"You're bleeding." His voice was gentle. "Do you have a first aid kit in that pack of yours?"

Hayley expelled her pent-up breath and nodded. "Any bars of service on that cell phone?"

"Nope."

"Too bad," she sighed. That meant her cell probably wouldn't have service either. A circumstance to be expected out here. As for the satellite phone, she had no idea what had been wrong with it at the cabin or if it would work now. She wasn't about to mention that she had the device with her to this guy until she understood the situation. "I'll get out the first aid kit as soon as I can persuade Mack to let me up."

"Far be it from me to touch your pack without permission."

Amusement colored his tone again, but it irked her less this time. Maybe his intentions were as good as they seemed. Then again, he'd invaded her property in company with a gang of criminals who'd tried to kill her.

He carried an automatic weapon just like those other lowlifes. Sure, he'd saved her, even opened fire on his pals to do it. But who were those guys, and why did this stranger go against them? His actions made no sense. She needed answers, and she needed them now.

Pressing a panting, wriggling Mack away from her, Hayley stood up.

"Go ahead and dig out the kit," she told the man. "It should be in the large front zipper pocket."

With a nod, the stranger turned away from her and knelt by the pack. His automatic hung benignly across his back as his fingers busied themselves with the zipper. Hayley swung her rifle free and positioned the stock against her shoulder. The barrel pointed straight between the stranger's broad shoulders. She clicked the safety off. At the sound, the man went still.

"Who are you?" Her shaky tone reflected the trembling that had suddenly seized her muscles. "And what is going on?"

Sean withdrew his hands from the small first aid kit he'd been reaching for and lifted them to shoulder height. He'd been expecting her questions to become demands at some point, but he hadn't wanted to start the discussion while they were in flight mode. And it would have been better to wait until after he'd seen to her injuries, but she'd chosen the timing, not him.

"I'm Special Agent Sean O'Keefe of the Bureau of Alcohol, Tobacco, Firearms and Explosives."

"You're a federal agent? What are you doing with a bunch of murderous crooks?"

"I'm undercover, ma'am. Or I *was* undercover to take down a weapons trafficking syndicate."

She huffed. "It's miss, not ma'am, and I'm sorry I messed up your operation. I wasn't doing anything but minding my own business when your bunch came along."

Her words came out in a tremulous rush, and he couldn't blame her for succumbing to nerves. She'd been shot at and had been forced to run for her life.

"Mind if I stand up and turn around?" he asked.

"Go ahead." The permission ended in an audible gasp like she was having trouble drawing a full breath.

Sean rose slowly and turned to face her. Her rifle was now pointed toward the ground, no threat to him, but her finger remained hooked around the trigger. She was shaking so badly it wouldn't take much to accidentally discharge the firearm. Two strides brought him to her. He took the weapon from her slack hands and flipped the safety on.

As he set the rifle to the side, the woman's knees buckled. Sean caught her in his arms and stopped her from hitting the ground. Her skin smelled of fresh air with a hint of something sharp and chemical like paint or stain. She wasn't petite in height, but she was slender and fine-boned. He'd call her fragile if he hadn't seen her in action and knew better. This woman had grit and smarts.

Her big brown eyes searched his face. "I don't know what's the matter with me," she murmured as he eased her gently to a sitting position against the sidewall of the cave entrance.

"A combination of mild shock and the ebb of adrenaline, I'd say." He offered a smile as encouragement. "Now you know my name. What's yours?"

"Hayley Brent."

"Pleased to meet you, Hayley Brent, but I'm sorry to make your acquaintance under these circumstances."

The woman nodded as she shivered and

tried to hug herself but winced at the movement of her hands.

"Here, let me zip up your jacket." Sean suited his actions to his words. "Any blankets in your pack?"

"There's a couple of M-Mylar emergency b-blankets."

Still using his cell phone flashlight app for illumination, he retrieved a blanket and draped it around her quaking shoulders.

"Okay. Let's get deeper into the shelter of this cave, and then I'll see to your wounds." He reached for her to help her up, but she shook him off.

"I can stand." She rose slowly and trod into the cave.

Sean followed her. The weak light from his phone revealed a rounded hollow in the rock roughly eight feet high and wide. How deep the cave went he had no idea. The illumination from his cell didn't extend that far.

Hayley settled herself on a low, flat rock near the center of the space, and her dog sat next to her, gaze alert. "You should save your phone battery," she said. "There's an LED camping lantern in my pack."

"Not much you don't have in there." Sean chuckled, and she responded with a weak smile. He rummaged around in the pack. "Too bad I don't see a ham radio." He found the lantern, clicked the button to activate the battery and the space brightened.

Hayley fixed him with a sober stare. "No ham radio, but will a satellite phone do?"

Sean's heart leaped in his chest. She had the device with her? Maybe he could still salvage this mess by calling in a team to stop the catastrophic arms deal that was about to go down and get Hayley and himself out of here in one piece.

"Where?" His voice emerged hoarse from tension in his throat.

"The largest side pocket."

With eager fingers, Sean turned the pack this way and that. There it was. The largest side pocket…with a bullet hole in the canvas. The breath vacated his lungs. Jaw tight, he undid the zipper, reached in and drew out the device.

"This satellite phone?" He turned and dangled the bullet-mangled mess toward Hayley.

She let out a deep groan. "That or the radio in my airplane is my only means of communicating with the outside world. The weird thing is, I tried to put out a distress call when you guys showed up, but the sat phone didn't have service."

Sean let out a grunt. "Patterson!"

"Who? What?"

"The leader of the merry band of thugs and thieves I infiltrated. Patterson's a gadget guy. As soon as he saw someone inhabited the cabin that we were told had been vacated for the winter, he flipped the switch on his military-grade signal blocker."

"Who told this crime boss that my brother and I were gone?" Her tone could have sliced rock.

Sean shook his head. "I don't know specifically. The grunts in his team aren't privy to the details of his intelligence gathering. I only know some contact of Patterson's in Fairbanks was watching the airport. The watcher must have been mistaken about seeing your plane come in. Whoever it was assured Patterson you were back in the city for the winter."

"That's disturbing." Hayley gulped audibly as Sean knelt in front of her with the first aid kit. "Your criminal boss's spy must be someone who knows Craig and me—or at least is familiar with our routine. I did bring my brother to Fairbanks so he could catch a flight for his writing assignment in Seattle, but a few hours later, I flew back to the cabin. I had a project to finish."

Sean studied the wounds on her attractive face and graceful neck. Thankfully, her eyes had been spared an encounter with shrapnel, and no embedded glass glistened in the minor facial cuts. Nothing seemed to call for stitches, and he didn't see more than a few dots of blood marring the shoulders and arms of her shirt. The padded vest showed torn spots, but it had offered some protection to her torso. Her hands and face had taken the brunt of the flying glass.

"Project?" he asked.

"I'm a chain saw carver." Hayley hissed in a breath as he dabbed disinfectant on small injuries.

"Really?" Sean paused in his ministrations.

"Hand me a chain saw, stand me in front of a giant chunk of wood and I'm a happy woman." Her heart-shaped face glowed and her eyes sparkled. Clearly, she took pride and pleasure in her craft.

Sean smiled. He couldn't help himself. Not only was her enthusiasm infectious, but she was easy to look at. With her delicate, clear-cut features and pristine complexion, she embodied a wholesome, girl-next-door beauty.

"Is everything okay?"

Her question brought Sean back to himself. What was the matter with him, staring as if he'd never seen a woman before?

"Not much is okay right now." He shook his head and dropped his gaze to examine her hands. Blood oozed from multiple cuts. He clucked his tongue. "We need to make sure these tools of your trade don't take permanent injury." Several glass shards stuck out from the tender flesh—a painful circumstance that made her scaling of the small cliff an impressive feat. "Tell me about your work."

She spoke enthusiastically with only a few groans and hisses interspersed with her words while Sean carefully removed the glass and disinfected the wounds, including the mild rope burns on her palms.

"There's one cut that should have stitches," he told her. "But we'll have to make do with a butterfly dressing."

"I'm a quick healer," she said as he began wrapping her hands in self-adhesive gauze. "Now, *you* tell *me* about the arms deal that got an ATF agent out in the middle of nowhere with no sign of backup. Or tell me I'm wrong, and you do have a team on the way."

Sean pressed his lips together. Sharp didn't half describe this woman.

"I wish I could say I have good news for you. As soon as I heard this deal was in the works, my handler had a team on standby. There was no reason to believe the meeting with the buyer would go down anywhere but in Anchorage, where Patterson's crew headquarters. I was wrong. This deal is so sensitive, the buyer insisted on a remote location and that abandoned way station next to your homestead fit the bill." Sean let out a long breath. "But I didn't know about the special arrangements until Patterson suddenly rousted his crew, including me, and stuffed us into an airplane. I had no time or opportunity to communicate with my handler." He met Hayley's bleak stare. "It looks like we're on our own."

Her gaze fell away from his. "We could run, but we're over a hundred miles southwest of Nenana. That's the nearest town. And the terrain between here and there is punishing, to say the least. There are no roads."

"What about other remote cabins out this way? Surely, someone between here and there will have a way to communicate with civilization."

Hayley shook her head. "I'm sure there are people living between here and Nenana, but there's no guarantee we'll happen upon them. That's all right. We probably won't have to try."

"What do you mean?"

"My brother was nervous about leaving me at the cabin alone. I practically had to force him out, but I finally persuaded him to go do his job as a journalist. I was only staying behind for a week or so. Still, he wasn't a happy camper, and that's why he calls every night to check on me. When I don't answer tonight, he'll alert his friend at the Fairbanks Alaska State Troopers' post. Someone will come out to check on me tomorrow morning."

Sean's stomach roiled. "The buyers are arriving in the morning, too. I have to get to the rendezvous site and stop the sale of the weapon."

"All this is over a single weapon?" Her tone conveyed skepticism.

Sean pressed his lips together. How much could he tell this woman? A few specifics within generalities would have to do.

"Patterson is selling the prototype and

plans for a new kind of stealth drone designed for the armed forces. The design and the prototype were stolen from the Anchorage-based company developing the technology. Bad people could do very bad things with the drone at the cost of a lot of innocent lives."

Hayley went sheet white. "Something like that should never get into the wrong hands."

Sean nodded but let out a long sigh. "If the operation had gone to plan, my ATF team was going to take down both the buyers and the sellers, put them out of business and retrieve the drone. As things have turned out, the best I can do is sabotage the sale. If someone flies in here to check on you tomorrow, Patterson's crew and the buyer's crew will hear them coming. But they're not likely to abort the high-value deal. Instead, they'll—"

"Ambush whoever shows up. I get it. We have to stop that from happening."

"Not 'we,' me."

"We." Glaring at him with narrowed eyes, she hefted her rifle. "I'm not hiding out in a cave while fellow Alaskans get murdered by lowlifes. And I'm certainly not standing idly by while greedy crooks sell a military-grade weapon to dangerous people." Sitting tall beside her slender figure, the dog let out a growling *woof.*

Sean's mouth opened, but no words came out. Just when he knew this assignment couldn't get any more messed up, the civilian he'd snatched from danger decided to go into battle beside him and he didn't know how to stop her. Especially since he badly needed her gun and her grit. But he'd never forgive himself if she got hurt on his watch.

# THREE

Sharp sparks of pain needled Hayley to groggy awareness. Her hands, her face and her right hip seemed to form the sources of the discomfort. What was going on? Memory flooded in along with consciousness. During an attack on her at the cabin, her hands and face had been struck by flying glass. But what was going on with her right hip? Where was she? A deep doggy snore beside her brought her fully awake.

Hayley stretched, the movement helping to identify the item digging into her hip. A small rock. She had been sleeping on her side beneath a Mylar blanket in a cave with her dog beside her. Last she remembered the stranger had gone to the cave's mouth to stand watch.

Where was the undercover ATF agent now?

She lifted her head. Only the faint glow of the moon and stars illuminated the cave opening. No aurora borealis at the moment. Though the season to enjoy the light show had begun this past month, the appearances were sporadic. The way sunrise worked this time of year in central Alaska, it would be nearly 8:00 a.m. before dawn's earliest light. There was no way for her to tell if it were the middle of the night or time to get up and get going for the day. A very precarious day if the risks discussed last night with the federal agent held true. As if she could doubt the danger after yesterday's aggressive attack.

Heart rate ratcheting up, Hayley struggled to a sitting position. Various injured and strained portions of her anatomy protested, and she let out a small groan. Mack stirred, blinking almond-shaped eyes at her. She ruffled the dog's thick scruff as her gaze scanned the area. She discerned a man-shaped shadow at the cave opening.

"Agent O'Keefe," she called softly.

The shadow figure turned. "I'm here." His tone was somber, but she could make out no expression on his face. "It's Sean, remember?"

"Sean. Got it. What's the time?"

"Going on seven-thirty. If you're up to it, or even if you're not, I think we should vacate this cave before it gets light enough for Patterson's crew to come looking for us. None of those guys are trackers. They're city boys, but they do know how to follow a blood trail, and you were leaving one."

"I won't be leaving one today." She rose to her feet, ignoring the minor aches of a night spent on the unforgiving ground. "And I'm ready to go."

"Good." A smile was in his tone. "Let's grab another one of those energy bars and a bottled water from your pack and then get out of here."

"Sounds like a plan." One of her body aches had indeed been in her stomach. They'd each eaten a bar, while Mack enjoyed a dog treat, last night before turning in—or at least before *she* turned in. "Have you been awake all night?"

"Not my first night with no sleep."

"Really? Too bad we don't have time to boil up some water and make coffee. I'm sure you could use the caffeine."

Sean shook his head. "I don't drink coffee." There was a degree of venom in the statement.

Either he truly hated the beverage or there was a deeper meaning to his words. Hayley gave a mental shrug. Now was not the time to pursue a trivial subject.

Ten minutes later, they were rigging the rope to let Mack down from the cliff. The malamute let out a high whine as they tied him into his makeshift transportation to the ground.

Hayley grasped his head between her hands and looked into his eyes. "It's all right, boy. We won't drop you. Be brave."

As if the dog understood her, he reached out his tongue and slurped her cheek. The attention tickled and a muted laugh left her mouth.

Lowering the dog down from the cave went more smoothly than lifting him up. A few minutes later, Hayley and Sean stood beside the animal on the forest floor. Their breaths left puffy clouds in the crisp, predawn air enriched by the distinctive pine odor of the boreal forest.

Now it was decision time. They'd argued to a draw last night about what was going to happen today. The ATF agent nearly matched her in stubbornness. But *nearly* didn't get the job done, as he was about to discover.

"I can't run away to save my skin." Hayley planted one fist on her hip. "I have to do something to warn whoever is coming to check on me today. That means I need to lurk close to my homestead and perhaps let out a warning shot as they come in. But you need to stop the weapon sale, which means a hike over to the abandoned way station where the buyer will land. Go! Don't worry about me. I have my rifle and Mack."

The tall, dark-haired man shook his head. "Not happening. I won't abandon you. Maybe we can figure out a way to accomplish both our goals without splitting up." Sean's white teeth showed in a grin. "I didn't sit up all night twiddling my thumbs."

"What do you have in mind?"

"Let's move away from this location as quickly and quietly as possible, and I'll fill you in. You lead since you know the area, but bring us back to your homestead in a round-about way. I didn't hear an airplane take off last night, so I have to assume Patterson's crew is still at your cabin."

"Makes sense," Hayley said, "if they intend to locate and eliminate us before they fly over to the way station to meet the buyers." She scowled and then her lips curved in a grim smile. "Toward the cabin is the last direction the crooks will expect us to travel."

"Great minds." The ATF agent winked.

A strange buoyancy filled Hayley's chest.

The guy might not technically be a crook, but she had no trouble imagining him as a heart-stealer. He was lethally attractive. Good thing she'd already learned her lesson the hard way when it came to handsome and dedicated law enforcement types. Too bad tragedy had come with the lesson. Her gut clenched.

Hayley brushed away the wrenching memories of her years-ago shattered engagement brought about by the needless death of her only sister. The eight-year-old grief could not be allowed to distract her right now.

"This way." She motioned toward Sean and led off the path they'd followed last night and into unmarked territory between the trees.

For long minutes, they made their way slowly and silently. At least, she and her dog made acceptably silent progress. Sean's was more moose on the loose. Branches snapped. Footfalls thumped. Not a good way to avoid detection by the men who hunted them or to approach the homestead by stealth.

Frowning, Hayley turned toward her companion. Dawn's advent had lightened the atmosphere enough for her to make out a blush on the ATF agent's face.

He spread his hands. "I'm a city boy, too.

Put me in a dark back alley, and you won't hear or see me coming."

"No camping or hunting in your background? That's almost un-Alaskan."

Hayley had intended the comment as light teasing, but Sean's face lost expression and his gaze hardened.

"Fishing is more my speed. My dad is a commercial fisherman in Portland, where I spent most of my childhood. I was born right here in the Alaskan bush but got yanked away from the wilderness when I was seven years old."

Curious choice of words to describe the situation of his early life. Yanked away? Hayley opened her mouth to ask the obvious question: *What happened when you were seven?* But then she snapped her jaw shut. Judging by the drawn look on his face, the subject seemed sensitive for the ATF agent and was none of her business. The two of them were essentially strangers. Comrades by necessity, but far from familiar friends.

"Okay, city boy," she said. "Here are a few Wilderness 101 lessons."

She showed him how to place his feet in a way that cooperated with the terrain and took advantage of the sound-deadening mulch of leaves and needles coating the ground.

"And press the branches aside with your hands," she told him. "Don't smash through them like a football lineman."

"Gotcha," Sean returned with that little amused grin of his.

Hayley's heart fluttered, and she turned on her heel. The first few steps onward, she violated every stealth lesson she'd given her student.

*Get it together, girl.*

She was the better part of a decade past that starry-eyed college girl who gave her heart away to a bad boy grin backed by empty promises. Her sister had paid the ultimate price for Hayley's faith in a guy with misplaced priorities. Now she was in a position that required her to trust another good-looking cop. Surely, lightning wouldn't strike twice, would it? This time it was her own life on the line.

Around ten minutes of stealthy progress later, Mack suddenly halted, turned his head and began to growl. Hayley hit her knees beside him and murmured a soft command to hush. The dog obeyed, but the latent growl vibrated against her hands on his thick neck and chest. Beside them, the ATF agent went still, his gaze fixed in the direction the dog indicated.

The sounds of snapping twigs and harsh male voices carried to Hayley's ears. At least a pair of men tromped through the forest less than twenty yards from their location. Mack's pointed ears stood at attention, and the rumbling in his throat gained volume. Hayley repeated the whisper for silence, and the noise subsided. A thump came, followed by a snarled curse. Someone must have tripped and fallen. The grumbling voices and sounds of clumsy progress through the woods continued for a short time, then gradually faded.

"I told you—city boys," Sean whispered.

"Following my blood trail like you said," Hayley answered, finally allowing herself a full breath. "This is our opportunity to make serious progress back to the cabin."

She led out, and the agent followed in her increasingly swift footsteps. What would she find when she caught sight of her place? Those creeps had better not have done more damage to the homestead that had been in her family for generations. They'd better not have hurt the carving she'd put her heart and soul into. With lives at stake, how foolish was she to care about an object? But she couldn't rein in the thought.

The trees began to thin, and a hand caught her elbow. Hayley slowed, and Sean came up close behind her.

"Don't forget Patterson will have some of his goons with him," the agent murmured.

"Right," she mouthed over her shoulder and modified her pace to a slow glide.

They reached the tree line behind and to one side of the cabin. At a motion from her, Sean took cover behind the bulk of a spruce tree, and she did the same opposite him. She commanded Mack to sit quietly beside her.

From this position, Hayley had a view of the side of her cabin and an oblique view of the front. The trespassers had found slabs of wood that they'd used to board up the broken picture window. Directly in front of them stood the rear of her workshop. In the growing dawn light, the back window revealed her eagle carving standing tall and strong. Hayley drew in a deep breath and let it out slowly. One small thing going right—but only if she had a chance to finish the work.

Movement by the cabin drew her attention. A man in work boots, chinos and a dark jacket stepped out the front door onto the porch, head swiveling in vigilance, assault rifle cradled in his arms.

"Crawford," Sean whispered.

Next, a man in a suit stepped outside, stretching his arms as if he'd recently awakened from sleep.

"Patterson." Sean's tone was a low growl.

At this distance, it was unlikely anyone in a building or the yard would be able to hear their soft communication over the swish of the breeze in the trees. A third man followed the suit, cuddling his gun in one arm.

Sean let out a snort. "Becker."

"Is he one of the men who shot at me yesterday?"

"The instigator no less."

Hayley's hands fisted. "He and the other lowlifes slept in a cozy cabin while we bunked in a cave. You said you had a plan. What's next, Special Agent in Charge?"

He sent her a grin with a teasing glint in his eye. "A peon fed is only a special agent."

"Not if you're in charge."

He answered with a nearly soundless chuckle, then quickly sobered. "A frontal shock-and-awe attack is out of the question. As soon as the shooting starts, the ones hunting us in the woods will come tearing back here and we'll be up against substantial fire-power. So, for now, we hide and watch. But as soon as a state trooper arrives to check on you, I'll lay down covering fire so you can get to them. Jump into that plane, get out of here and call for help. I'll stay behind and stop the sale by any means necessary."

"But what about—"

A distinctive steady buzzing noise from overhead interrupted Hayley's protest. Heart rate kicking into overdrive, her gaze searched the sky. No plane in view yet, but one was on the way.

"Someone's coming," she whispered urgently to Sean. "Is it the buyer?"

The agent shook his head. "Too soon."

"Then it must be whoever my brother sent."

Hayley's airway tightened. Was she really going to abandon Sean here while she was whisked away? What choice did she have? Would she even make it to the rescue plane in the first place? There was a lot of open space to cover between here and the lake. That depended on God…and Sean's aim. And once the call for more help went out, would reinforcements arrive for Sean before he was cut down in service of his country?

So many questions and uncertainties. Hayley met his dark gaze. Steady. Determined. Solid. He'd shown himself to be a man of action and courage. She shouldn't start doubting now. But she didn't have to like it. She jerked a nod in his direction and returned her attention to the sky.

A Cessna floatplane came into view, clearly intending to land on her lake. Hayley's heart jumped at the Alaska State Troopers' symbol painted on the side of the aircraft. A single person occupied the cockpit. Then the plane disappeared from view on the far side of her workshop, but a splash indicated a touchdown.

Hayley's pulse quickened. Surely the officer was sharp enough to note that the large plane parked at the dock opposite her small Cub lacked a tail sign. Someone in uniform would know what that indicated. Maybe the person wouldn't be entirely unprepared, but she needed to be ready to back them up. And she needed to be ready to run for it when Sean gave the signal. Hayley hefted her rifle and flipped the safety off.

She took a step forward, but Sean clamped a firm grip around her arm.

"Wait!" he said, tone sharp. He gestured toward the three men on the porch of her cabin.

The new plane's advent hadn't caused so much as a ruffle in the suited man's fancy hair. The one Sean called Patterson and his two goons stood nonchalantly watching the landing as if law enforcement arriving in the middle of their illegal operation was no big deal. A minute later, a husky man dressed in an Alaska state trooper's uniform trotted toward the trio on the porch.

"I'm sorry, Mr. Patterson," the trooper called out. "I had no idea Craig's sister was still out here. What did you do with her?"

Hayley's mouth went bone dry, and the breath caught in her lungs. "I know that trooper." Her voice came out in a hoarse whisper. "That's Glenn Cauley, my brother's friend. Craig is going to be heartbroken."

The full import of the situation burst in upon her, and blackness edged her vision. No one was coming to help them. No one even knew there might be trouble at her homestead, because the one her brother had trustingly called was a traitor to his badge.

Sean's jaw clenched. Nothing boiled his blood as much as a crooked cop.

Worse, there was no getting Hayley out of here, and the number of guys and guns against Hayley and him had increased. When the pair hunting them in the woods came up empty, they'd return here. And then when the buyer arrived within the next hour with who knew how many more goons, stopping the sale would truly be hopeless. They had to do something *now*, and the risks were enormous.

Correction. *He* had to do something now.

A bandaged hand fell on his arm. "We need a new plan."

Sean looked down into Hayley's expectant face. "I'm open to suggestions." His tone came out more of a snarl than he liked, but she didn't even blink at his harsh tone.

"As you said, a direct attack on the cabin is out of the question. We'd both end up dead in a hurry. But what if we blow up Patterson's plane with the drone in it? That would end the dirty deal right there."

A tiny bit of tension ebbed from Sean's gut. "I like the way you think. You don't happen to have any dynamite laying around, do you?"

"Nope." A taut smile bloomed on her lips. "But if—say—a rag soaked in wood stain and set alight were stuffed into the plane's gas tank, the result might be the perfect *kaboom*." Her smile faded. "Only I'm not sure how to make that happen without the saboteur getting shot or blown to bits as well."

Sean pursed his lips and let out a soft hum. "If the torch is rigged and inserted right, the explosion won't happen instantaneously. It will take some time for combustible fumes to build up. Someone will have to cover the other when they sprint for the plane. How are you with that rifle?" He nodded toward the Winchester in her grip.

"Good enough to keep them ducking for cover."

"All right, then." Sean blew a long breath out his nostrils.

With the temperature still hovering around freezing, the exhale formed contrails of cloud in front of his face. He still didn't want Hayley involved in this dangerous business, but he didn't see a way around including her.

"First," he said, "we have to get through the rear door of your workshop without being seen."

"And here's our opportunity." She gestured toward the cabin.

Sean's heart rate pegged up a notch. Patterson, his bodyguards and the trooper were going into the cabin together, but they might not stay inside long. Soon, one or more of them would likely step outside to stand guard.

"Let's move." He led out across the lightly frosted grass at a slow lope, weapon at the ready, and pointed toward the cabin. If any of the crooked gang inside caught a glimpse of them, Hayley and he would be finished. At least the boards over the main window minimized one possible viewpoint, though they could certainly be seen from other windows.

Sean sped up, and footsteps on his heels assured him Hayley followed with the dog panting in her wake. The workshop sat at right angles to the cabin, and at last, they reached a spot where the building shielded them from view. No outcry of discovery had greeted their movement.

A few strides later, they reached the back door and Sean turned to allow Hayley to let them into the workshop. Hand on the knob, she spared him a glance. The bright color on her cheeks stood in sharp relief to the pallor washing the rest of her face. Her chest heaved with breaths more labored than the short sprint warranted. Fear always magnified exertion. Yet her gaze held only steady determination that defied the fear.

With a brief nod, she pulled open the back door of her workshop and they darted inside. The interior was significantly warmer than outside, but the air was laden with scents of wood shavings and pungent finish. Several sizes and styles of chain saws lay across a long workbench. Behind the bench, a wall of neatly hung tools stretched across one side of the building. Cement covered the floor and wooden rafters buttressed the high ceiling.

But the object that occupied the center of the cavernous room left Sean's eyes wide and his mouth agape. Impressive didn't begin to describe the eagle carving. His gaze caressed every inch of the magnificent work of art. Hayley not only enjoyed her craft, but she excelled at it.

Tearing his attention from the piece, he settled his gaze on the artist. "Wow!"

The anxiety on her face morphed into a flush and a slight smile. "Do you like it?"

"The word 'like' is too tame." He shook his head. "I'm in awe."

A scowl formed on her brow. Had he said something wrong?

"Then you can understand how *annoyed* I am to have my work disrupted by a crew of crooks." She tossed her head, brown ponytail swishing. "That was sarcasm through understatement, by the way."

Sean rumbled a soft chuckle. "Then it's only fair we *annoy* them back."

If the situation weren't so dire, he'd almost characterize their interaction as fun.

"Let's get busy," he said, sobering.

Only minimal communication proved necessary as they duct-taped a pair of paint stir sticks together to provide sufficient length for their makeshift torch. The unlit end would be inserted into the gas tank, allowing a buildup of escaping fumes that would eventually ignite the fuel and hopefully lead to a flaming kaboom. Next, they soaked a rag in stain, wrapped it around an end of the stick and secured it with more duct tape. Hayley produced a lighter from her seemingly bottomless backpack.

Sean took the lighter and the makeshift torch in one hand and hefted his weapon with the other. "I think we should switch guns," he said. "The Winchester Featherweight is an outstanding rifle, but with only five rounds in the magazine, you won't do well against an automatic."

"Agreed." Hayley nodded.

"Do you know how to handle an auto?"

"How hard can it be? Point, sight, press trigger."

Sean offered her a half smile. "Point and press trigger might be more accurate. The bullets spit out too fast for sighting to do any good. Just sweep the muzzle across the area you want to target. Anything in the way will take a hit. I'm going to set this on semiauto, which will give you three-bullet bursts, so you *will* have to press the trigger more than once. If I leave this on full auto, you'll run out of ammo too quickly to hold the gang at bay for any length of time."

"Got it." Hayley's throat pulsed, indicating a deep swallow.

Sean's heart panged. He was asking a lot of this innocent bystander. No doubt she'd never aimed a gun at a human target before.

He laid his hands on her shoulders and looked into her eyes. She didn't look away. "Whether you hit anyone or not," he said, "the purpose is to pin them down until I reach Patterson's aircraft. At that point, your Cub and the trooper's plane will offer some cover for me. I'll stab the stick end of the torch into the tank, then light the rag end. It'll take a short time for the fire to ignite the fumes and reach the fuel. Lay down cover fire until I get back to the workshop."

She nodded, still holding his gaze without

a flinch in her resolve. He released her and handed over his assault weapon, along with an extra magazine. Then he slung her rifle over his shoulder. Grim-faced, she turned toward the nearest window facing the cabin and turned the crank to open it a crack. Now she could shoot without shattering the glass.

"Before I light the torch," he said with a hand on her tense shoulder, "I'm going to untie your Cub and push it away from the dock. Even so, there's no guarantee that every aircraft in the vicinity won't go up in flames, but at least that one might survive and offer us a radio to call for help or even a way out of here if we manage to subdue Patterson's crew."

Her thin smile advised him she wasn't fooling herself with the possibility that the two of them would take down the thugs arrayed against them, but the immediate objective was stopping the sale of a cutting-edge weapon to evil people. They would roll with the circumstances that followed achieving the objective. He'd settle for escaping once again into the forest. With Hayley's wilderness savvy and supplies, they could survive for quite a while.

She gestured toward a door on the far side

of the workshop. "I'm going to put Mack in the storage closet, so he'll be well away from flying bullets. Then I'll take up a position behind the thick support beam flanking the side window that faces the cabin."

"Good plan." Sean nodded. "As soon as you're in position, I'll race for the dock. Don't open fire until you see a response from the cabin."

"Understood. Let's do this," she said, lifting her chin.

Sean leaned in close to her—close enough to appreciate the depth and purity of her velvet-brown eyes. "If things don't go well for me, you take Mack and get out of here. Run as fast and as far as you can."

Hayley's somber gaze scanned his face as if she were memorizing it. "I don't plan to fail, Mr. Special Agent."

The intensity of her words shot a tingle up Sean's spine. He stood straight, a grin splitting his face.

"Not failing. Sounds like a terrific plan to me."

He turned on his heel and strode toward the front door of the workshop. A scrabble of doggy claws and the soft creak of a door told of the malamute finding shelter in the closet.

Sean stopped at the door with his hand on the knob and looked over his shoulder. From her window battle station, Hayley offered him a solemn nod.

Go time.

Sean sucked in a deep breath, opened the door and burst into a run. He was completely exposed. Any stride could be his last. His life depended on God's grace…and the courage of a woman he'd only just met.

# FOUR

A sharp pain stabbed through Hayley's fingers. She caught her breath and stared down at her hands. Her knuckles around the weapon shone white. Releasing air from her lungs, she eased her grip and the pain subsided.

*Steady now*, she told herself. *Eyes on the prize.*

Hayley returned her gaze to the cabin. No movement...yet. Sean was out the door and on his way to the dock, his footfalls against the packed earth faint and growing fainter.

Suddenly, the cabin door flung open, accompanied by a shout. Reflex drew Hayley's finger taut around the trigger. A sudden burst chattered from the weapon in her hands, sending her heart rate into the stratosphere. The yelling from the cabin turned into a yelp, and the door slammed shut. Lungs heaving, Hayley blinked rapidly against darkness edging her vision and pressed the trigger again. Her bullets smacked into the porch.

Gunfire erupted through chinks in the boards across the cabin's broken picture window. Dull thunks signaled bullets hitting the workshop's outer walls. Nearby windows shattered in a hail of glass falling like sparkling crystals around Hayley's shoulders. A squeak left her tight throat and she instinctively changed position, even as she pressed the trigger again and again.

Gunfire from the cabin ceased. She must have successfully driven the smugglers into taking cover. Exactly the result desired. But how long could she keep these well-armed crooks at bay? And how close was Sean to completing his assignment?

Never mind. She needed to concentrate on keeping the coast clear for him to blow up that plane.

*Please, God, help him do what he must and get back here safely.*

Then what? Run like startled deer? But where would they go? No time to ponder the next steps. Here and now needed all her concentration.

At a flash of movement from the cabin door, Hayley sent another trio of bullets into the porch. Whoever had been there withdrew once more. She inhaled a stuttering breath. Did military combat feel like this—hope and terror roiling the gut, clarity and confusion battling in the mind? This small taste was more than enough for her to appreciate afresh the brave men and women who served on the front lines.

A burst of fire from the cabin sent a round of bullets thudding into the side of the workshop, but no more broken glass. The gunmen had to be firing blind through any window opening. The shooting seemed aimless. More to rattle her and draw her attention than hit her. To what purpose?

Abruptly, a spate of gunfire erupted from another location in the cabin. The bullets seemed to be flying from one of the second-floor windows on the side facing the lake, probably from her bedroom. The big negative to the smuggler's position was her inability to respond to the attack because the shooter was out of sight and protected by thick cabin walls. The big positive was the oblique angle for the gunman to attempt hitting Sean running on a straight path between the dock and the workshop. Not that they wouldn't try though, and once the ATF agent left the dock, there would be a few yards when he would be quite exposed to that angle of fire.

Too bad Hayley had no way of knowing where in the sabotage process Sean was, and when he would be the most vulnerable. She clenched her jaw. Nothing for it but to create the most nuisance and racket she could.

Hayley continued pressing the trigger, sending round after round through the empty picture window and into the cabin walls. Not that the latter would penetrate, but the smack of the bullets had to be unnerving for the crooks in the cabin. All at once, the press of her finger brought only a hollow click. Out of ammo. How had Sean shown her to switch out the clip? Hayley's mind scrambled as she fumbled to reload.

A cacophony of fire from the cabin ripped bullets into the workshop walls and sent glass flying. With a high-pitched shriek, Hayley ducked behind the workbench.

*Steady, girl*, she ordered herself.

Hauling in deep, regular breaths, she brought her trembling under control and at last seated the fresh clip into her weapon. At a lull in firing from the cabin, Hayley popped up and returned fire. This back and forth couldn't continue much longer. She was rapidly using up the last of the ammo for the automatic.

A familiar, throaty blast sent a shiver through Hayley. Her rifle. Sean must be returning fire on whoever was shooting from the second floor. Did that mean he was on his way back to the workshop? Had he succeeded in the sabotage plan? How frustrating in this life-or-death situation to know nothing for sure.

Heart hammering against her ribs, Hayley resumed the repetitive pressure on her weapon's trigger. Then that hollow click sounded again, and her lungs went vacant. She was out of ammo. Nothing more she could do.

A barrage of gunfire slammed into the workshop, and Hayley sought cover once again behind the workbench. Curled into a tight ball, heat from her gun's barrel radiated against her cheek.

How could she endure one more second of this horror? What choice did she have?

Gunfire drizzled away. Silence rang in Hayley's ears. She held her breath.

Where was Sean? Was he okay? Or was he lying forever still on the moist Alaskan earth?

Behind her, Mack erupted in a flurry of sharp barks. His heavy body began slamming repeatedly against the closet door panel. What did he hear or smell that she couldn't? Maybe Sean was back from his mission. Catching her breath, Hayley turned her head toward the workshop's front door.

A mighty slam sent a shiver through Hayley's body. Then her insides froze.

Not the front door. The back.

She swiveled on her heels and switched the direction she faced. A burly man stood framed in the open doorway. Not Sean and not one of the men from the cabin. The dark-clad figure had to be one of the smugglers who'd been hunting Sean and her in the forest. They'd known those guys would return to the homestead as soon as they heard gunfire, and they must have hustled to be here so quickly. At least this guy did. Was his partner close behind?

A death's-head grin bloomed on the man's face as he raised his gun toward Hayley. Rivers of ice flowed through her core. A splintering crash sounded from the direction of the closet, and a massive bullet of fur and fangs burst toward the gunman. The smuggler shouted something unintelligible and began to swivel his gun barrel toward the canine attacker.

"No!" Hayley shrieked and instinctively propelled herself upright in a lunge toward the threat to her dog.

Not that their efforts mattered. There was no way either Mack or she were going to reach the gunman before bullets swept the room, ending them both.

Charging through the workshop's front door, Sean had no time to aim the rifle. Just shoot before that deadly auto in the enemy's hands went off. The rifle blast echoed through the cavernous room even as the bullet struck the smuggler Sean knew as Clete Seaton. The man staggered backward. His spray of automatic fire peppered the metal ceiling like a clatter of hailstones. A second shooter, Arlen Bates, appeared behind the first, scowling like thunder and brandishing his weapon.

"Get down!" Sean shouted.

But Hayley's momentum carried her into a waist-high tackle that slammed Clete to the floor with her on top. The dog ignored the pileup and, with a mighty snarl, leaped over the struggling pair and into the face of the second gunman. Arlen went down under an eighty-pound mass of snarling canine.

Sean pounded across the room, dodging the spread wings of the carved eagle. Hayley struggled on the floor with the first gunman. Both pairs of hands gripped the automatic weapon in a quest for control. Sean was certain his bullet had struck the man, but it couldn't have done much damage because Clete didn't seem to be bleeding and he was about to win the battle for the gun. Mack was well in control of the tussle with Arlen, gripping the man's arm securely in his teeth as Arlen thrashed, letting out high-pitched screams.

For the moment, Sean ignored that struggle and skidded to a halt beside Hayley and Clete. The smuggler rolled, pinning Hayley to the floor. Sean seized the opportunity to smash the butt of the rifle into the back of Clete's head. The smuggler went limp, and Sean flung the man's bulky body away from the brave woman who'd taken him on without hesitation.

Sean stared down into Hayley's wide eyes. Her chest heaved for breath as she tried to sit up. He put out his hand and helped her rise to her feet.

"Get his gun." Sean motioned toward Clete, then moved immediately onward to address the struggle between Arlen and Mack.

Not much of a struggle. Arlen lay on his back, covering his face and neck with his arms as the dog continued to savage him. Sean scooped up the automatic weapon Arlen had dropped when the malamute barreled into him.

"Easy, Mack." Hayley's voice came from behind Sean.

The dog released his jaws from his prey but remained atop the man, continuing a deep belly-growl. Arlen whimpered and curled into a fetal ball, redness soaking the arm of his jacket.

"The fire didn't work to blow up the plane?" Hayley asked.

Sean turned toward her. She gazed back at him, pale and shaking, but Clete's gun hung from the crook of one elbow. The weapon was useless, however. Apparently, Sean's bullet hadn't hit the smuggler, but struck the gun, distorting the barrel.

"We'll know any second," Sean answered Hayley. "It takes time for the gas fumes, the gasoline and the flame to interact into an explosion. Right now, we need to get out of here. Ditch that gun." He pointed to Clete's ruined weapon. "But grab the extra ammo from him and get your pack." Hayley scurried to comply as Sean acquired extra clips from Arlen and kept the man's gun. They were going to need all the firepower they could get.

As Sean bent over him, the agonized man glared up at him. "We're going to kill you," he snarled.

"You can try, but we don't plan to let you." Sean turned toward Hayley. "Let's go!"

He pointed toward the wall of forest. Hayley took off, Mack at her heels. Sean followed, his feet barely on the move when bullets strafed toward them from the cabin. Dirt puffed up from the ground too near their fleeing figures for comfort. Then the trees enveloped them.

No explosion yet. Sean's chest tightened. Had he run the gauntlet to the dock in vain?

The next moment, a great whoosh seemed to suck the oxygen from around them, and then a crump of explosive energy swept a wall of air toward them like a tsunami. If the workshop building had not shielded them, they might have been thrown off their feet despite the tree cover.

Sean stumbled but kept on going, a grim smile tilting his lips. There would be no illegal weapons sale today. They'd won that fight but the battle to stay alive continued.

Patterson was a vengeful man. He and his

crew wouldn't simply head home with their tails between their legs…even if they could get one of the other planes into the air, which might not be possible after an explosion like the one he and Hayley had engineered. The boom had been bigger than he'd anticipated. It was possible, but not guaranteed, that all the aerial transport was now inoperable.

Too bad they couldn't have stuck around to assess the damage and possibly access one of the aircraft radios at least. Now they were fleeing without means of communication with the outside world, an advantage that belonged solely to Patterson. Would the guy call in reinforcements? Almost certainly. Their little trio—man, woman and dog—needed to put as much distance between the smuggling crew and themselves as they possibly could. Hopefully, investigating the results of the explosion would slow their adversaries down.

Sean hustled to come level with Hayley. "Are you hurt at all?"

"No," she puffed out. "You?"

"Good to go."

"Then we'd better get to gittin'." Her word choice flirted with humor, but her tense expression let him know she was aware of the likelihood they would be hunted.

Sean spared her a smile. "Great work back there."

"You, too." A grin flickered across her lips.

"Any ideas on which direction we should head?"

"We're moving on the straightest path toward the nearest settlement."

"Over a hundred miles away."

"Yup."

Nothing more needed to be said. She'd explained the difficulties of the journey facing them. With armed bad guys nipping at their heels, they would have to face and overcome those difficulties one obstacle at a time.

# FIVE

Hayley stumbled over a tree root, righted herself and hurried onward, forcing her feet and legs to keep a swift pace. The adrenaline shakes were on the ebb, leaving her thoughts sluggish and her limbs weighted. If only she could collapse onto the soft, mossy ground and take a long nap. Maybe she would wake up to discover the violence and turmoil of the past sixteen hours had been nothing more than a bad dream.

She let out a snort under her breath. Denial was an exercise in futility. Keeping her mind focused on the next actions for wilderness survival was the only way forward now.

Mack trotted easily along beside her, his panting breaths soft but clear in the morning stillness. Sean's footfalls behind her were steady if still a bit forest-newbie with snapped twigs and grunts when he clumsily navigated a branch in his way. Good thing they weren't out on a hunt. But in time he'd learn to move quietly. He'd have to. They were the hunted, not the hunters. A chill quivered through Hayley.

"We should stop soon and hydrate," Sean said.

"Agreed, but I'm out of bottled water. I have a canteen, but it's empty. Normally, when heading into the forest I would have had time to fill it at the house. That wasn't an option this time." She shrugged, and the heavy pack dragged against the movement. "There's a stream about a mile from here. We can stop then."

"Sounds good. Let me carry the rucksack. You've hauled it long enough."

Hayley wasn't about to protest that suggestion. They stopped and she handed over the pack. Loss of the extra weight afforded her a second wind as they hurried onward. Her perked ears caught no telltale sounds of pursuit.

Could she hope the smugglers would give up on them now that their big weapons deal was thwarted? Hayley firmed her jaw. She was being delusional again. Sean and she were witnesses to illegal activity. From the way Sean talked about this Patterson guy, the smuggling kingpin didn't sound like someone who would tolerate liabilities.

The terrain began to dip mildly and then severely, slowing their pace as they picked their way carefully. The loamy ground was slick with fallen leaves and needles, so they frequently steadied themselves with their hands against tree trunks. Soon, the shush of slow-flowing water reached Hayley's ears. A few steps later the ground leveled off, and they stepped out of the trees onto the bank of a small creek. The water was shallow and glassy clear, revealing a stony bottom. The far bank lay only a few yards distant.

Mack crouched by the flowing water and lapped eagerly. Sean stepped ahead of her and squatted at the edge of the creek. He scooped a handful of sparkling liquid into his palm.

"Ouch. Cold," he said, carrying the water toward his mouth.

"Don't drink it." Hayley stopped him with a hand on his shoulder.

Sean gazed up at her with lifted brows. "The water's not pure out here? I don't see how that can be."

She stifled a grin. "It's as pure as nature makes surface water, I suppose, but it still contains all sorts of rotted vegetation, debris and bacteria that our civilized stomachs aren't equipped to handle."

"Yuck." Sean dumped the water back into the stream.

Hayley chuckled. "I'll fill the canteen and put a purification tablet inside. We should be able to drink it in about a half hour. It'll taste pretty awful, but it will be safe. When we make camp tonight, we can boil water, or if we can't risk starting a fire, I have a micro-filter and charcoal purifier we can use. Those options will taste better."

Sean stood up and wrinkled his nose. "I'll leave you to it, then."

"Give me the backpack, please."

He handed it over, and she knelt at the creek-side. The process of finding the needed items, filling the canteen and adding the puri-fication tablet took only a couple of minutes.

Hayley stood, gripping the full canteen, and gazed solemnly into Sean's dark eyes. "How serious will that gang be in pursuit of us?"

"A heart attack would be less serious."

"I'd already come to that conclusion." She sighed. "But you know these guys better than I do." She compressed her lips and dropped her gaze. "I had hoped…" She let her voice trail away.

"Hang on to hope." Sean laid a sturdy hand on her arm. His warmth comforted if his words didn't. "We've survived thus far, and none of those guys have wilderness smarts like you do."

"My brother's traitorous friend, State Trooper Glenn Cauley, does. He's an expert tracker and a dead shot. I should know. Craig and I have gone hunting with him."

Sean released a long, whistling breath. "We'd better get going, then."

Hayley jerked a nod, turned and led the way into the shallow creek. At first, the water swirled only a few inches up her thick hiking boots, the waterproofed leather holding the moisture at bay. A few steps later, she reached a deeper stretch about a yard wide and took a leap beyond the portion that would have topped her boots and soaked her feet. The cold water splashed onto her jeans, chilling her legs, but hiking would soon warm her and dry the moisture.

They stepped up onto the far bank and reentered the tree cover. Now that they'd put several miles of distance between them and their enemies, and with the morning only half-gone and a long day's walk ahead of them, she moderated their pace to a brisk walk.

"This trooper friend of your brother's has got to be really sweating the situation," Sean said. "If Patterson insists on him acting as a tracker for his crew, he won't be able to return to his station. Questions will be asked."

"How could he return to his station with his plane disabled?"

Sean stepped up to walk nearly level with her. "Neither of us got to see the results of that explosion. I have no doubt the plane carrying the stolen drone was toasted and sunk. Your plane that was tied up on the other side of the dock almost certainly took some damage. But there wasn't room for a third plane at the dock. When Trooper Glenn landed, he drove his floats up onto the beach and threw out an anchor. From our perspective in the forest behind the workshop, we weren't able to watch him do that. I didn't know it until I left the workshop, but that's why I think it's possible his aircraft is operational."

Hayley halted and glared up at him. "You're just now telling me this?"

He shrugged. "We haven't had much chance to chat."

"Fair enough." She continued walking. "If I were Glenn, I'd call in some pretext for not returning to his station right away. Troopers out here have *lots* of territory to cover. Then I'd call my brother and lie through my teeth that his sister is fine. No worries." Her voice became a snarl as she finished her hypothetical narrative. If blood could literally boil, steam would be erupting from her pores.

"Spot on analysis, I'd say." Sean fell back as they came to a section of thick forestation that allowed only single file progress. "But either of those actions will only be a delay in your brother and outside authorities discovering something is wrong."

"Yes, but by the time legitimate search parties are sent out, we'll be so deep into the wilderness we won't be found unless we help them find us with a signal fire or something obvious."

"And a signal fire would attract the bad guys, too. Makes me think running might not be the best plan. Maybe we should let them catch us."

Hayley halted and whirled toward her companion. "Lack of sleep must be warping your thought processes. Those guys have a lot more firepower and more numbers than we do."

Sean spread his hands, palms up. "I'm not saying we confront them head-on, but a little subterfuge might help us snatch a satellite phone. We'll have to isolate someone with a phone, incapacitate him and take it off him."

Her heart did an extra *ka-bump*, and a small grin formed on her lips. "You mean like a trap?" Hayley's smile faded. "But who among them has control of the satellite phones? Logic tells me Patterson will have brought one for his crew, and I'm sure Glenn has one."

Sean frowned. "It'll be next to impossible to cut Patterson out of the pack. His guys will be all around him—if he even hazards his designer shoes to wilderness trekking. He's more likely to direct operations from the cabin, and he'll keep his sat phone with him."

"That leaves Glenn with the other phone, and he has razor-sharp wilderness awareness." Hayley huffed. "Isolating and incapacitating him will be like cornering a wolf."

"Then we'll have to outfox the wolf."

"It will be dangerous."

"Everything about this situation is dangerous, but I'm not about to let anything happen to you. I *will* get you to safety someway, somehow." Sean's gaze locked with Hayley's, his sable-brown eyes fierce and intense.

An odd sensation went through her, equal

parts warmth and unease. The man was too appealing for her peace of mind. Sure, she trusted him to do everything in his power to protect her. After what they'd already been through together, how could she not? But this unwelcome attraction to a man wedded to a career in law enforcement could not be entertained. Her former fiancé Ryan's misplaced priorities had cost her the life of the only other sibling she and Craig had possessed. The hole in their lives still yawned deep and wide.

Hayley shoved the dark thoughts away. She needed to remember that Sean had already risked his life and exposed his undercover status on her behalf. Didn't that prove he put people before mission? That he wasn't like Ryan? An internal shudder rolled through her. No, she dared not soften toward him in any personal sense. The risk to her heart was too great.

Hayley drew herself up stiffly. "I know you'll do your best, but life is uncertain. I learned that a long time ago." She forced a smile that might have come out more of a grimace. "We'd better put more distance between them and us if we want to have enough time to stop later and plan an ambush."

She whirled on her heel and marched off through the trees. Did she spy a mix of hurt and confusion on his face? Maybe, but he didn't know her history, and now was not the time to explain her reaction. If that time ever came.

Sean plodded along behind Hayley and her dog, his gut churning. What was with her mixed warm and cool signals? And why did his insides turn to jelly at the thought of her coming to hurt? He prided himself on remaining calm and in control in tricky situations. Such a temperament was essential in the undercover game. But the very idea of violent criminals harming Hayley stabbed unreasoning fury through him.

Could the reaction connect with what had happened to his mother all those years ago when he was a boy? His terrible, costly carelessness? Sean's gut clenched and his teeth ground together. That was then; this was now. And the situation wasn't at all the same. Sean physically shrugged the swarm of memories away.

*Stay focused.* He caught an evergreen bough and pushed it out of his way as he walked on, his boots passing softly over the loamy ground. Maybe he was getting better at wilderness trekking. Just not as good as the woman blazing the way. His gaze followed the slender, graceful figure ahead of him.

Hayley didn't need his help with wilderness survival, but maybe the depths of his protective instinct had been triggered by the fact that she'd proven as committed as he was to sabotaging the sale of the drone. That impressed him. And she had courageously kept him alive during his sprint to blow up Patterson's airplane. He wasn't used to people having his back. Operating solo was also a part of undercover work.

The woman had grit and heart, and he admired those qualities. She was appealing with that wholesome, girl-next-door vibe. Not that he hadn't been around attractive women. But this particular one tugged at his heart in a way he'd never experienced before. He'd have to get that reaction under control and maintain his cool. A calm and rational head was a necessity if they were to have any chance of survival. They were also going to have to conserve their energies and regularly take in whatever food and water they had on hand or could forage. The foraging bit would be mostly on her shoulders.

"Do we have a fine-dining destination in mind for lunch?" Sean asked, forcing a light tone.

Hayley stopped and turned toward him, a small smile playing on her lips. "Destination? Yes. But I doubt the cuisine will rate so much as a star."

He let out a low chuckle. "My stomach couldn't care less about stars."

"How about you tide over that appetite of yours with a little of this?" She held the canteen out toward him. "The water should be safe to drink now."

"You first."

"Skeptical of those pills I put in here?" Hayley quirked an eyebrow.

"Not at all." He shook his head. "Must be my inner gentleman peeking out."

She grinned, and Sean's heart somersaulted. Disheveled and with pine needles strewn in her hair, he had to admit this woman was more attractive to him than any other he'd ever met.

"Your mama must have raised you right," Hayley said.

A pang tore through Sean. The smile forming on his face soured. "I'm sure she would have if she could have. She passed away when I was seven years old."

Hayley's expression sobered. "I'm sorry to hear that. Is that why you and your dad moved away from Interior Alaska?"

"That, and—well, never mind." He shrugged. "It was a long time ago."

No amount of time would be long enough to forget the screech of tires and the tortured wail of twisting metal. Or the shrill screams of his mother and himself as the vehicle flipped end over end. And nothing could erase the knowledge that the accident had been his fault. Kind people had told him he wasn't responsible, but he knew better. His father knew better. The man had made sure his son understood his guilt was why his mother's family had never again wanted anything to do with him.

Hayley's gaze went soft, and she shook her head. "You never really get over the loss of someone so close to you. And maybe we shouldn't want to get over it completely. The pain helps keep the memories alive. I should know."

Tension bled from Sean's muscles. At least she wasn't going to pry more deeply into the story. He'd like to preserve whatever good opinion this woman might have of him. "There's some wisdom in that statement. Who was it for you? A parent?"

Her gaze went cool and distant.

"I'm sorry," he blurted. "I shouldn't have asked." Sean mentally kicked himself.

"No, *I'm* sorry. Asking the question was a normal response. My grandparents passed a few years ago within months of each other, but my parents are fine and living in Texas." Her conscience pricked against the disingenuous answer, but mentioning her twin sister, Kirsten, would bring too much pain to deal with at the moment. She unscrewed the cap on the canteen and took several swallows. "Here."

Hayley handed him the canteen, and this time he accepted. The water had a chemical tang that wasn't pleasant, but it was wet and satisfied his thirst. He returned the container, and she attached it to the ring on her pack that was designed for that purpose.

They moved on but shortly came to a break in the trees. Hayley made a motion to halt, and Sean crept up beside her. A large patch of open ground faced them. At least an acre of wild grasses rippling like brownish-green waves in the chilly breeze.

"I'm more comfortable keeping to the cover of the forest but going around this meadow will cost us precious time. What do you think?" Hayley's gaze met his.

She was asking the wilderness tenderfoot? He frowned and scanned the treeless area.

"I say we should go for it. I doubt Patterson and his thugs could possibly be close enough to spot us."

She nodded. "I haven't heard any sounds of pursuit. But more importantly, Mack hasn't signaled any."

Her fingers ruffled the hair on the dog's head. The animal gazed up at her with adoring eyes. Sean's heart lightened. They had a pretty good team going here. Back at the homestead, they'd succeeded together in a dangerous operation to destroy the stolen drone before it could be sold. Together, they could succeed in fending off Patterson's crew and either reaching safety or calling in rescue. He had to believe that, or they were done before they'd gotten a good start.

"Let's hurry," he said.

Hayley nodded and broke tree cover with him on her heels and the dog romping ahead. Out in the sunlight, the temperature rose significantly. Still cool, but pleasantly so.

"Watch where you put your feet," Hayley told him. "The last thing either of us needs is a twisted ankle from stepping in a ground squirrel hole."

"Gotcha, Girl Scout," Sean answered with a chuckle.

She tossed him a mock scowl over her shoulder, and he laughed.

A spate of barking from Mack drowned the merriment. Hayley halted, gripping Sean's arm. She shushed her dog with a command. The animal quieted but stood stiffly at attention, ears pricked, moist black nose pointed toward the sky.

"He hears something," she said. "Listen."

Sean stopped breathing and strained his ears. A distant, throaty hum caught his attention.

"Airplane," he murmured to his companion.

Hayley nodded. "It could be Glenn's plane out looking to locate us, or maybe someone else who could possibly be of help?"

"I think we need to assume the former is more likely."

"Agreed."

Sean looked both ways, behind and before them. They'd reached the middle of the open area and would have the same distance to cover either direction they chose to go. The buzz of the plane engine grew steadily louder. They didn't have much time to reach the woods before being spotted.

"Run!" Hayley cried, surging toward the far side of the meadow, rather than back the way they had come.

Sean raced after her, amazed at Hayley's speed. He wasn't having to hold back much to maintain his position on her heels. The woman was in seriously good shape, but the lifestyle out here, as well as her chainsaw-carving profession, would tend toward significant exercise.

The tree line grew steadily closer, but so did the airplane noise. Sean darted a glance toward the sky. No visual yet of the aircraft, but that circumstance could change in an instant. Ahead of him, Hayley suddenly stumbled and then staggered to keep herself from falling face-first to the ground. Likely her foot had found a ground squirrel hole. Nearly impossible to watch for those when running full out.

Catching up to her, Sean snagged her around the waist with one arm and swept her forward beside him. She was limping now. Must have twisted her ankle. But he couldn't allow an injury to slow them down. Sean dug deep into reserves of speed and charged toward the forest, bearing much of her weight. A step before they reached cover, he looked up again.

There it was. The trooper's plane, definitely. And whoever was aboard had a clear view of the meadow. Another stride and the trees swallowed them.

Had they been spotted? If so, their enemies would have their location. There was no way to know for sure, but the answer could spell the difference between life and death.

# SIX

Even allowing Sean to take some of her weight on himself, hot pins stabbed Hayley's ankle as she forced herself to keep hobbling onward. She gritted her teeth against outcries as they wound through the trees. Mack had slowed and now trotted beside her injured leg, occasionally brushing against her thigh as if lending support. The dog's dark eyes kept darting up toward her face, and a soft whine issued from his throat.

"I'll be okay," Hayley told him and spared a pat on his head.

The softness of Mack's thick fur lent an odd comfort to her. Her touch and gentle words must have done the same for him because his whining ceased.

The buzz of the airplane engine traced in a circular motion overhead. Did that mean they'd been spotted? Hayley's chest constricted. How close to their location were the ones who pursued them on foot?

Sean edged nearer to her. "Is there another cave or something nearby where we can hole up and take a look at that ankle?"

His question jerked Hayley out of her worry cycle. They'd deal with their pursuers when they must. Now was time for them to concentrate on gaining distance. Her injured ankle might slow them down but couldn't be allowed to halt them.

"No need to stop for triage," she said. "My ankle's not broken…at least, I don't think so. A sprain probably." She continued to hobble forward, leaning into Sean. The initial stabbing pains were subsiding into a deep ache. "Leaving my boot on is the best support my muscles and ligaments could receive."

Sean let out a soft hum. "Good point, but getting that leg elevated would also help, which is not—"

"Possible right now." Hayley finished the sentence for him, then nearly bit her tongue over the accidental return to the annoying habit they'd started at their first meeting. Hopefully, he hadn't noticed. "No worries. If we stop for a minute, I can dig out the painkillers and anti-inflammatory analgesics in—"

"The first aid kit." Sean winked.

Yup, he'd picked up on the habit and perpetuated it on purpose. Hayley suppressed an eye roll as he brought them to a halt and slid the pack off his shoulders.

"Listen," he said and went still with his hand on the pack's zipper.

Hayley held her breath and perked her ears. The wind rustled tree branches, evergreen needles and leaves. Near at hand, a soft *rat-a-tat-tat* betrayed the presence of a woodpecker. No other sound caught her attention.

Her gaze met Sean's. "The plane is out of earshot. What does that mean?"

"Either we were spotted, and our location has been reported, or we weren't seen, and they've gone to search elsewhere. I'd give my left arm to know which one is true."

"They? You think more than one person is up in the plane?"

"Patterson's pilot and Patterson himself, probably, in a temporary foray from the cabin that won't dirty his shoes. I can't see him ruining his designer suit on a trek through the Alaskan bush. That's what he has his goons for."

Hayley crinkled her brow. "Surely, if we'd been located, this Patterson guy would have tried to stay nearby and watch for signs of us breaking cover as we travel."

"I hope you're right." Sean pulled the first aid kit from the pack. "But we should plan for the latter."

"Agreed." Hayley accepted the pills from him and swallowed them with a little water from the canteen. "I have a destination in mind. It's at the outer limits of the area I'm familiar with, but it should offer both shelter and perhaps an opportunity to ambush our pursuers."

"How far?"

"Miles yet, and the terrain's about to get a little challenging. Also, we'll have to pass through a sizable open area of marshy ground."

Her companion frowned, glancing down at her foot.

Hayley put a hand on his arm. "We can do this. We have to. I'll be fine to hike without support as soon as the meds kick in."

"Then let's take a few minutes and let the pills work." He motioned toward a fallen log, and they sat down. "What's for lunch?"

Hayley dug in the pack and came out with packages of trail mix, featuring dried fruit and berries, as well as nuts and seeds. "You don't have a tree nut allergy, do you?"

Sean shook his head, and she handed him a package. Then she brought out a canine meal bar for Mack.

They finished their meal quickly and stowed away the empty packages.

Sean rose, gazing down at her with his brow furrowed. "How is the ankle?"

Hayley shook her head. "I won't know until we get going, but it's not like we can stay here."

"Okay," Sean huffed. "Let's get moving."

He held out his arm, and Hayley took it. The man was sturdy as a tree. She glanced up at him as they moved along. Sean's chiseled profile would look authentic on one of her carvings featuring native people, yet his name was entirely Irish. There was a backstory here that he'd shied away from explaining. Not that his ancestry was any of her business. Curiosity, however, was a perennial feature of her personality that often drew good-natured teasing from her family.

The pain in her foot ebbed into a faint ache, and she began to stride on her own. They could make good time now, provided she watched her step. The terrain here in the Alaskan bush was largely flat or rolling with occasional steeper grades. If she took those with care and moderate speed, she should be okay.

However, soon the trees thinned, and Hayley's skin prickled with the sensation of being exposed to the watching eyes of violent enemies. Her gut told her to hurry, but the ground under her feet would not allow speed as it became mushy and then marshy. Every footfall came with an audible squish and a slight splash of water against their boots. The earth seemed to suck at them, reluctantly releasing each foot from its grip. Hayley's ankle began to throb, but she tucked her lower lip between her teeth and pressed onward.

"Are we in danger of sinkholes?" Sean asked.

She shook her head. "No, but the muck might get worse before it gets better."

He answered by taking her arm once again, and she let him. As they progressed, his head tilted upward, gaze searching the sky, as much as it tilted downward, watching their steps.

"Mack will warn us if the plane approaches again," she told him softly.

"Right." Sean let out a brief chuckle. "It's not like we have any place to hide in the middle of a marsh, anyway."

"Stop!" Hayley called abruptly, her breath catching. Slowly, she squatted down and scanned a grassy hummock poking out of the thin coating of water.

"What is it?" Sean's words came out thin and strained.

She pointed toward an enormous paw print in the earth. "Bear. Probably a male, judging by the size of the paw. And the print is fresh. We'd best proceed with caution. Bears are ravenous this time of year, eating as much as possible before hibernation. We need to do our best to steer clear of the one that's in the area."

"Great!" Sean snorted. "People want to shoot us, and bears want to eat us."

Hayley rose and offered him a wry smile. "Don't leave out the hungry wolves."

"Ri-i-ight. I guess that makes us equal opportunity prey."

"It makes us dangerous prey." She patted her rifle. "But I'd rather avoid having to shoot at anything at all."

Sean gave a soft chuckle. "We're of one mind on that subject."

"Turn around and let me get the bear spray out of the pack. Hopefully, we won't have to use that either."

Hayley retrieved the spray, and Sean held it while he offered his arm to her again. She took it, and they proceeded, gazes scanning the terrain. The water eventually rose to lap around their ankles, sending a chill into her bones, but at least the waterproof leather of Hayley's boots kept her feet dry. She assumed Sean's boots were doing the same. They looked to be good quality like hers. Mack trotted ahead of their slow progress, then circled back around them, big head on a swivel, constantly sniffing the air.

"That's a protective dog you have there," Sean said.

"Partly it's a breed thing, but partly it's Mack's big heart and high intelligence. Craig and I figure he's exceptional for his kind, but then, we're in love with the guy."

Hayley grinned up at Sean, and he answered the smile. Her heart performed a little jig. If ruggedly handsome had a quintessential model, she was looking at it. But more than outward appearance, warmth and intelligent strength gazed back at her. Like Mack, but in a human being.

She tore her gaze from his as her dog trotted up to them, a low growl rumbling in his throat. The malamute halted in front of them, muzzle pointed toward a large creature shambling through the marsh. At this distance, the animal appeared little more than a brown blob of fur, but given the direction human and beast were traveling, their paths would soon meet.

The wild animal showed no signs that it had spotted them yet, but that could change at any moment. Then massive jaws loaded with sharp teeth and paws armed with razor-like claws, all packaged in hundreds of pounds of muscle and bone, would confront human frailty. Any other time of year, and Hayley would expect the bear to flee if people acted right. Now, with winter snows and arctic cold impending, such an expectation might be optimistic. Sean, Mack and she could soon be in a primal fight for their lives.

Sean's heart thudded against his ribs, and his breath came in short spurts. Put him in a small room with armed thugs, and his pulse would barely spike. But he had no clue how to deal with a wild creature that could shred him with one swipe of its paw. Maybe the beast wouldn't notice them. Forlorn hope with the three of them standing out in the open like this.

"How well do bears see?" he muttered at Hayley, never removing his gaze from the lumbering bear.

"About the same as humans, but their sense of smell is better than a bloodhound's. Thankfully, the wind is minimal, not blowing our scent toward him. Uh-oh."

Sean's throat constricted. The bear had stopped its shambling forward movement. Its massive head lifted, and it appeared to be staring straight at them.

"Get the bear spray ready in case of attack," Hayley said softly. "You can depress the nozzle when he's about sixty feet away. If that doesn't work, I'll use the rifle as a last resort, even though a gunshot might attract the attention of our pursuers. But first, I'd rather try warning the bear off before we need to use either the spray or the gun."

"Warn off a *bear*?" His words came out with a wheezing quality reflective of the tightness of his throat.

"Just stay still," she said. "Any sudden movement or attempt to run could trigger him to charge. Bears can run up to thirty miles per hour for short distances, so we wouldn't get far."

"Yikes!" Sean hissed between his teeth.

Abruptly, the animal reared up on its hind legs, gaze still fixed on the strange invaders to its territory. The creature was enormous, far taller than Sean's six feet, and the outstretched front limbs would have no problem wrapping around any of their bodies and tearing them to bits. The air vacated his lungs, and a deep growl rolled from Mack's throat.

"Easy, boy," Hayley told the dog. "Stay." Then she lifted her arms high. "Hey, bear, bear, bear," she called in a loud voice that seemed to echo across the cavernous open space.

"You're inviting him to come over here?" Sean glared at his companion.

"Rearing up like that signals curiosity, not aggression," she said. "He needs to perceive us not as prey or as a threat, but as an aberration in his environment best avoided."

"Will that work?"

"No clue."

The bear dropped down to all fours and began to accelerate toward them.

"I guess not," she said. "Get ready."

Sean fumbled with the safety on the bear spray nozzle. Who would believe he was about to use aerosol spray against a bear? How did that even work? Like pepper spray on a human?

The animal had already cut the distance between them in half. Sean released a burst of spray, but Mr. Bear didn't so much as break stride.

Suddenly, Mack burst forward, barking and growling.

"No, Mack!" Hayley screamed.

But the dog didn't slow his charge toward

the threat. His protective nature had over-ruled her verbal restraints.

Hayley lifted the butt of her rifle to her shoulder, then let out a strained huff. "I've got no shot. Mack's in my line of sight."

As the snarling dog closed in on the bear that was easily several times his size, the wild animal slowed and veered away slightly from the humans even as it roared and swiped a massive paw in the malamute's direction. Mack danced out of reach and began circling the bear, darting in to nip at the animal's heels with every revolution.

"Hold off on the spray," Hayley called, and Sean halted his finger halfway into depressing the nozzle once more. "You'll get Mack, too."

The dog's thick figure disappeared around the far side of the bear, and Hayley lifted her rifle. The gun roared once and then again. The bear seemed to jump, and then it whirled and began running obliquely away toward the tree line. Mack followed, barking and growling.

Hayley called for her dog and the animal halted, turned and began trotting back toward his human companions, tongue lolling. In people-terms, Sean would describe the stride and tilt of the malamute's head as nothing less than triumphal.

Hayley handed Sean the rifle and squatted to wrap her arms around her dog's neck. "You bad dog," she murmured, but the tone belied the words and the animal awarded her a face lick.

Sean busied himself with reloading the rifle. "I don't think you hit the bear."

She rose to her feet, one hand still buried in Mack's ruff. "I wasn't trying to put a bullet in the big fellow. Just scare him. Though if the animal had persisted in his attack, I would have been forced to shoot him and pray for a clean kill, both for the bear's sake and for ours. A wounded grizzly is one of the most dangerous creatures on the planet. That was way too close for comfort."

"You're telling me!" Sean studied his companion.

He was quaking on the inside, but her face had washed pale and her body visibly shook. The next moment, her knees appeared to give way and she was falling. Sean swept out an arm and caught her, then drew her close. She folded into him, a soft sob leaving her throat. He wrapped both arms around her, and she gripped his jacket in fisted hands, face buried against his chest.

Silent seconds crept past as the tremors

gradually faded from her body. Tension ebbed from Sean's muscles. He closed his eyes, and the world narrowed to the two of them clinging to each other. A refreshing vanilla-spice scent wafted to his nostrils from her hair. What would it be like to hold this woman as something more than an act of comfort in a dangerous situation?

Then she stiffened and pushed away from him. His arms went vacant. The loss struck him like a blow to the gut, but he didn't reach for her.

Sean shook himself mentally. He couldn't afford to be distracted by his attraction to Hayley. Neither of them could indulge romantic fantasies when the here and now demanded their full attention. Not that she'd given any indication of viewing him as anything more than a comrade in arms, united against mutual danger.

"We'd better get across this marsh and into tree cover again," she said briskly, her fingers swiping at moisture on her cheeks.

"Let's do it," he answered and reached for her arm to offer support.

She turned and stepped away from him, avoiding his grasp, and marched toward the forest, hardly a limp in her stride. Mack followed at her heels, darting a glance over his shoulder at Sean. The animal's dark eyes sent a message: *mine, not yours.*

*Gotcha, buddy.* Sean mentally acknowledged the canine memo and followed the pair.

His gaze swept the area, but there was no sign of the bear or any other wildlife. If those gunshots had spooked a bear, all other more skittish creatures would be making tracks far away. That couldn't be said for the two-legged hunters on their trail.

Sean understood the necessity of discharging the rifle and could only be grateful for its effectiveness against the bear. But, if their pursuers hadn't already been informed by the airplane pilot of the direction their quarries were traveling, and if they were within earshot, the rifle reports would have betrayed their location. Patterson's crew could be homing in on them this very minute.

Sean lengthened his stride and caught up with woman and dog. "I think we should hurry to find cover."

"Agreed," she said and stepped out more briskly.

The marshy ground still sucked at their boots, but the standing water had all but disappeared. As one, they broke into a trot.

Hayley's gait betrayed a hitch, but she never slowed as they neared the forest.

Behind them, a human shout rolled across the marsh. The hairs on the nape of Sean's neck stood to attention. As much as he craved to look back and identify the location of the threat, the way forward over uneven hummocks of moss and grass demanded his focus. Neither of them could afford the delay of a fall or further injury to a limb. Reaching the trees was their only hope of survival.

Sean allowed Hayley to draw ahead and placed his body between her and their pursuers. A few strides later, her slim figure disappeared past the wide reach of a squat, sturdy evergreen. Sean surged forward between that evergreen and the stately aspen next to it. A branch near his head suddenly snipped off the pine tree even as a gunshot reverberated through the crisp air. Ice surged through his veins. The next bullet could easily have his name on it.

# SEVEN

Glops of mud fell away from Hayley's boots as her feet flew over solid earth, but just as the squishy muck had slowed her pace, now the necessity to dodge around trees impeded her progress. At least the trunks and branches offered cover from flying bullets. The shooting abruptly ceased, and she slowed. Mack's panting was loud in the stillness, but where was the thud of Sean's boots?

Hayley stopped and turned around. No Sean. Her heart skipped a beat. Had he been hit? Darkness edged her vision. She forced herself to stop holding her breath and inhale. The blackness receded. Pulse throbbing in her ears, she inched back toward the marsh. Would she discover Sean lying in a puddle of blood?

An automatic weapon suddenly blasted. Not from across the marsh, but right here in from of her. A scream tore from Hayley's throat, and she froze as if she'd turned to a block of ice. The gunfire ceased as abruptly as it had begun.

Silence descended. Then footfalls. Sean's tall, sturdy figure burst into view.

Hayley let out a little squeak. "Why are you grinning?" Her tone came out a growl.

"It's my go-to response when I put the bear scare on the bad guys."

"The bear scare? I take it you didn't hit anyone."

"Just like you and your bear." Sean proceeded past her, still grinning.

Hayley stomped after him. "You startled me out of my socks, mister. I thought you might be dead and then suddenly you're blasting away. What for?"

"Believing we're waiting for them to step out of the tree line so we can take them down will make them think more than twice about crossing that strip of marsh after us."

"But we're not waiting."

"Nope."

A reluctant smile grew on Hayley's lips. This ATF agent was sharp. "You bought us some time while they debate their next move. Genius! My head hadn't gotten past the running part."

"Now is the running part." He stepped up the tempo of his strides, and she mimicked him.

A strong mile passed beneath their scurrying feet. Then they stopped, panting, for sips of water. Despite the profound chill in the air, rivulets of sweat trickled down Hayley's back underneath her jacket.

"We can't keep going at this pace," she told Sean.

"Agreed. I—" His words were drowned by a cacophony of distant gunfire sounding at their rear.

Hayley shuddered. "What's that about?" With a wrinkled brow, she looked at Sean.

His lips thinned. "I assume, after some arguing, our pursuers decided not to lose the time it would take to find a way around the marsh. They simply plowed straight ahead, guns blazing, to keep us from returning fire if we were still waiting there for them to show themselves."

"So, they're going to discover soon that we didn't hang around, and they'll be on our heels again."

"True, but their decision also means they will use up a lot of ammo for nothing."

"A good thing, right?" Her heart lightened.

"For sure. Any ideas now for evasive tactics?"

"That's been on my mind." She began to increase the pace. "We'll come to a stream soon and head upriver in the water, which should make it difficult for Glenn to stay on our trail."

"Won't they already have guessed we're going to head in the direction of the nearest civilization? What did you say that town was? Nenana?"

"That's just it. The stream we'll be in doesn't lead to Nenana. The water's origin is in the Brooks Mountain Range to the north. Us taking the water route will be counterintuitive for our pursuers. They'll waste time looking for our trail."

Sean frowned as he strode beside her. "Won't taking us off course cost *us* precious time?"

"Our time won't matter if we're shot dead." She darted him a stern look.

"Fair point. Lead on."

Hayley jerked a nod and adjusted their course. A soft chuckle reached her ears.

She let out a snort. "First you're grinning and now you're laughing?"

"Can't help it. Patterson's boys are muscle-bound gym rats. Aerobic training isn't macho enough for them. They've got to be struggling for breath like fish out of water. A part of me wishes I was a bird in a bush watching all the huffing and puffing and whining."

Hayley turned her head and scanned him up and down. "You've got muscle, but I take it you're not allergic to aerobic exercise."

He shrugged. "The crew liked to tease me about rabbiting around the local park, but I've always found that jogging clears my head."

"Good thing for us, then. If we can keep up this pace, we can run them off their feet. Well, everyone but Trooper Glenn Cauley."

"But he's one guy."

"The guy who can keep tabs on us and figure out a way for the others to take a shortcut to intercept and ambush us."

"Cheery thought." Sean grimaced. "We've already determined that Cauley and Patterson must be in possession of satellite phones so they can keep in touch even if Glenn scouts ahead. Another reason why we need to figure out a way to get our hands on one of those phones."

"For now, let's deal with throwing them off our trail and finding somewhere to hole up when the sun goes down. They won't be able to travel safely in the darkness any more than we will."

Hayley's next step landed in an unexpected dip and shot an arrow of pain up her leg. She let out an involuntary huff.

Sean hooked a hand through her elbow and brought them both to a halt. "How is your ankle?"

The limb was hot and throbbing, but she wasn't about to turn into one of the smuggler boss's whiny crew. Not when there was no choice about staying on the move.

"I could use more painkillers and anal-gesics. Then I'm good to go." She forced a smile.

"Right." Sean lifted skeptical eyebrows.

Hayley took her medicine, and they both hydrated from the canteen. Then they each grabbed a strip of jerky to gnaw on while they traveled. Mack snapped up a doggie treat she offered him. It was important to do all they could to keep their strength up. The terrain roughened, and few words were spoken as they navigated.

Half a mile later they came to the stream and halted along its beach of mud and shale. Hayley studied the flow. The water rushed deeper and faster than the creek they crossed that morning, and the bottom of this one was rocky and uneven. Not optimal. With a sigh, she knelt and filled their depleted canteen.

Then she rose and faced Sean. "We have two objectives here. One, don't venture in so deep the water goes over the tops of our boots. The last thing we need is freezing wet socks. Two, remain far enough from the bank that we don't splash water onto it, which will give away our route to Glenn's tracker eyes. Oh, and I guess there's a third requirement." She gazed into Sean's dark eyes. "I'm sorry, but you'll have to carry Mack because staying long-term in the water will be too cold for him, and he'll leave paw prints on the bank."

"Done." Sean's solemn gaze matched hers. "I'm up for it."

"I believe you, but he's heavy. Step onto that flat stretch of shale on the bank when you pick him up, or your footprints will dig unnaturally deep into the ground."

Sean moved onto the rock, squatted and called the dog's name. Mack left the bush he was sniffing and trotted to the man. Sean's arms reached to encircle the dog, but the animal twisted away. Hayley spoke a few stern words to Mack, and Sean's second attempt to pick him up succeeded. The ATF agent grunted as he heaved to his feet with his load. His face reddened with the effort, but he showed white teeth in a jaunty grin.

Sean clearly had a bit of macho in him, too. If only she was fit to at least carry the backpack for him, but she was going to be challenged enough with her bum ankle to wade through the rough, rock-strewn water without support. A long breath left Hayley's lungs, emitting small contrails of condensation. With dusk drawing in upon them, the temperatures were dropping to around freezing.

Firming her jaw, she turned away from the agent and stepped out. The shallow torrent immediately transmitted chill to her feet through tough leather and thick socks. How long they could wisely remain in the water remained to be seen.

For long minutes, they struggled upriver against the current that tugged at their feet and on uncertain footing over slick rocks. Speed was not an option here. Mack began to emit a steady, high whine.

"Easy, boy." Hayley spoke gently to him over her shoulder.

The animal's head was up, nose pricked. Her gut clenched. Were their pursuers within scenting distance already? How could that be? She increased their speed as greatly as she dared. Behind her, Sean's breathing was starting to come in deep puffs.

"Not much longer," she said.

Suddenly, a large animal heaved to its feet from among the tall bushes lining the waterway. The young, female moose let out its characteristic moaning cry and turned tail, its shaggy coat becoming flashes of black among the trees and brush.

Behind Hayley, Mack's whine changed to a growl and then a full-throated bark. She swiveled barely in time to witness her dog lunge from Sean's arms into hot pursuit. The lunge sent the ATF agent sprawling backward into the creek with a great splash.

Hayley's heart plummeted to her toes. Their situation had gone from deep distress to the verge of disaster. Unless they stopped to build a fire and dry Sean's clothing, hypothermia would quickly claim his life. But if they stopped, bullets would soon end both their lives.

In a single moment, Sean's body went from mildly chilled to arctic—like being swallowed whole by an iceberg. The reflexive impulse to escape the sensation shot him to his feet as quickly as he'd fallen. Shivers stabbed through him as he slogged onto the riverbank.

"We have to light a fire and get you close to it immediately," Hayley said, following him onto land.

Sean shook his head as he removed his sodden stocking cap and gloves and thrust them into water-beaded jacket pockets, where they would soon freeze solid. "We can't s-stop." His chattering teeth made him stutter.

"I know, but we have no choice. You'll die."

He turned toward her. Hayley's face had washed pale, and her eyes were huge as her gaze swept him up and down.

"I'll be uncomfortable, but I won't d-die," he said. "At least, not quickly. My legs, head and hands took a dousing, but my waterproof j-jacket kept my torso dry. As long as my core stays warm, my limbs will function if we keep moving briskly. We can stop and light a fire when night falls. Our pursuers will have to do the s-same."

Hayley nodded, and color returned to her face. "For a city boy, you came prepared with good gear for wilderness survival."

Sean managed to force his frozen cheeks into some semblance of a smile. "A northwestern fisherman's s-son wouldn't buy any other kind of jacket than w-waterproof."

"All right, then. Let's get trotting before your jeans freeze solid. We're only a mile or so from the abandoned cabin I wanted to reach before nightfall."

"A c-cabin? Right n-now, that sounds like a dream come t-true."

Hayley darted away into the bushes and the forest beyond. Sean followed, trudging at first against the resistance of the freezing pants. Ice chunks snapped and broke off with every stride. Then the resistance loosened and he managed a lope, although the wet fabric chaffed his legs with every stride. The effort kept his core warm after losing the coverings for his head and hands turned discomfort into misery he must ignore. He wouldn't be surprised if his hair and beard sported icicles. Not that he was going to try to verify the presumption with fingers steadily going numb.

Hayley was right. He needed to get cozy with a fire very soon.

For some time, the terrain remained flat but sparsely wooded. Sean kept vigilant with his head turning this way and that, but he spotted no other humans. Hopefully, Hayley's ploy of confusing their trail with the river

Then Hayley turned and a large sheet enveloped his body. The Mylar blanket. Gentle hands urged him to a seat on the floor. Reality faded, and he drifted in a pale haze, not awake, but not unconscious either. Dimly, he registered brisk movement around him and someone putting the dry socks on his feet, but he no longer had the power to move. Gradually, blackness took him.

Warmth. Not the false warmth of advanced hypothermia, but genuine heat. Also, a crackling sound, and from somewhere near his nose, a crisp pine scent. The latter as much as anything had awakened him.

Sean opened his eyes and turned his head slightly. The movement brought a crinkling sound and a heightened pine odor. He was resting on evergreen boughs and covered with one of the Mylar blankets. Sean's gaze found the primary source of warmth—the fire dancing in the great hearth mere feet from his prone body.

Hayley! Where was she?

Sean raised himself on his elbows from the pine bed and spotted a form wrapped in silvery Mylar blanket sitting at the far side the hearth. Her injured leg was elevated

had bought them enough distance from their pursuers that the thugs wouldn't get within eyeshot of them before they all were forced to stop for the night.

Mack soon appeared, trotting along, tongue lolling. Sean sent him a glare the dog countered with a tail swish and an expression Sean could only describe as smug at chasing away the frightened moose.

About a mile later, another splotch of dense woodland swallowed them in stands of spruce, aspen, birch and pine. The trees cut the wind and rendered Sean marginally warmer. The relief was tempered by the necessity of a slower pace. His fingers—and his toes, too, since his socks had gotten wet— were in danger of frostbite. That fire couldn't happen soon enough.

"We're close now," Hayley said.

Sean pushed himself faster even as he forced his unfeeling fingers to ball and flex. He had to keep some circulation going. Why did he feel so tired? As if he wanted nothing more than to curl on the ground and let sleep take him? Sure, he'd gone overnight without sleep, but he'd skipped a night's rest before and not felt as if he could barely put one foot ahead of another. Creeping hypothermia.

Had to be. He couldn't allow the encroaching blackness in his mind to take him.

Had…to…keep…going.

Then they stepped out of the trees into a small clearing surrounded by woods. Sean blinked and forced himself to focus. The building sitting in the center of the open area barely deserved the name shack. The entire structure leaned in one direction and the porch had deteriorated so much it no longer connected to the cabin. One thing it had though, was a sturdy stone chimney, and a pile of chopped logs was stacked near it.

"Let's get inside." Hayley gripped his jacket, tugging him forward.

Sean took a step and stumbled. Standing still had been a mistake. His legs would barely function, and his body began to shudder.

"Get moving, mister!" Hayley's harsh shout echoed in his ears as if coming from a distance. "I can't carry you. You have to walk."

A sharp sting penetrated the numbness in Sean's cheek. He reared back, hauling in a deep breath. She'd slapped him.

*Good girl. Now, move, boy!*

Sean forced his wooden legs to move and his leaden feet to plod forward. With ach-

ing slowness, they crossed the yard, onto the rickety porch and stepped the door into the musty murk of the ancient interior.

On robotic feet, Sean allowed Ha lead him close to the cavernous heart only thing missing was the one thin could save him—a roaring blaze. B brain couldn't seem to tell his body h go about starting one. He was shutting d Not good.

Hayley knelt and worked his boots then turned and dug through her pack. S swayed where he stood but couldn't figure o how to slump to the floor against the pressure of his frozen jeans around his legs.

"Get out of those wet pants and so Hayley's voice came to him as if from tance. "And put these on. Do it now!"

Her bark galvanized him into slug tion as she shoved a pair of dry lon and socks at him. She turned away mage farther in her pack as Sean r complied with her order, the wet j ping and crackling as he wrestled The long johns were a bit too sm hugged him with welcome wa the socks on was beyond him.

on a chunk of firewood, the other one curled close to her body. Well, she wasn't really sitting. More like slumped, eyes closed, against the stone chimney surround, as if she'd been awake and keeping watch, but gradually slumber had gotten the better of her.

Mack lay near Hayley's feet, but at Sean's movement, the dog lifted his head. The animal seemed to grace Sean with a doggy grin and then resettled his great head onto his large paws and closed his eyes.

Sean also settled himself again. Hunger and thirst niggled at him but responding to those needs was too taxing. Weariness weighted his whole body and mind. Not surprising considering the exertions they'd undergone since he landed with Patterson's crooked crew at Hayley's homestead deep in the Alaskan bush.

After his mother died in the accident, and his father took him away to Portland to start work on a fishing boat, Sean had never thought to return to this part of the state. This was his mom's home stomping grounds where he'd spent his earliest childhood. Mom had been a constant then and his dad was around daily, rather than the arrangement in Portland of leaving Sean with his brother's family while he spent weeks and even months at sea.

Those early memories of Interior Alaska were vague, like faded and out-of-focus pictures. But they were overlaid with a sense of peace and contentment he'd never experienced since the day his childish antics triggered the greatest tragedy his life had ever known.

Sean shoved the searing memory away. As often as the terrifying recollection had swooped upon him—sometimes at the most inopportune moments—he should have learned by now there was no point in reliving the past. And no absolution either.

He gathered the Mylar blanket close to his neck and turned onto his side, facing away from the fire, and let the darkness claim him. But the refuge of sleep betrayed him, and the dream came. Horror swallowed him whole.

# EIGHT

A keening cry jerked Hayley awake. She sat up straight, and her stiff muscles complained at the sudden movement. Mack reared onto his haunches with a whine. They both stared at Sean, who thrashed on his bed of pine boughs, letting out wounded groans.

Was he ill? Did he have a fever?

Hayley scrambled forward on all fours and placed her hand against his forehead. The skin was warm but not unnaturally so.

At her touch, Sean lunged into a sitting position. His eyes popped wide, and a yelp exploded from his throat. Hayley scooted backward, and Mack stood on all fours with a bark that subsided into a soft growl. Hayley's heart pounded against her ribs.

Sean's chest heaved. Then he seemed to shake himself and the expression of vacant terror faded from his gaze. He blinked at her and Mack. Slowly, lucidity returned to his look.

His squared shoulders slumped, and he pinched the bridge of his nose with a thumb and forefinger. "I'm sorry. The last thing I wanted to do was wake you."

Hayley huffed. "I'd say the last thing you wanted to do was experience whatever dream was turning you inside out."

Sean's mouth quivered in what might have started to be a smile but turned into a frown. "Can't argue with you there." His tone was thin as a blade.

The wrenching sadness in his gaze twisted Hayley's insides. Mack padded forward and swiped his tongue against Sean's cheek. The man let out a shaky chuckle and ruffled the dog's fur. With an inexplicable lump in her throat, Hayley turned away and busied herself with feeding a few more logs onto the waning fire. Sean's dream had to have been about something intensely personal and painful.

She settled close to the blaze and drew her blanket around her shoulders, knees pulled close to her torso. The weathered old cabin didn't do well at holding the outdoor cold at bay. Occasional wind gusts infiltrated gaps in the wallboards and tousled the flames in the hearth, even as it nipped at exposed skin.

Hayley swiveled toward the ATF agent. He was looking at his watch. A waterproof variety, of course.

"It's almost five a.m.," he said. "Since we bedded down around the time the sun went down, we've actually had a decent night's sleep. But it won't get light out for hours yet, so we'll have to stay put for a while."

"I wonder how our pursuers are faring."

Sean smiled. "I doubt they're enjoying four walls around them—such as they are." He gazed around at their rough surroundings.

Hayley managed a light chuckle. "You don't adore the luxury accommodations?"

"Oh, I do." Sean grinned and the last of the nightmare shadows fled from his face. "I'd go so far as to call this fancy little shack a lifesaver…and you, too. Thank you. I would have been a goner without you."

His intense brown gaze burrowed warmth into her heart. She bit her lip against the impulse to ask about the dream that ended their night's rest. The question would be intrusive, wouldn't it? Then again, maybe there was something she should know about since they were fleeing for their lives together. Silence fell as Hayley rearranged the burning logs with a stick, sending sparks floating onto the blackened hearthstones and urging the flames to greater heights.

"I'll tell you," Sean said softly.

Hayley's jaw slackened. How did this guy know she had a bad case of the curiosities?

"But I'd like a drink of water first," he said. "My throat is dry as sandpaper."

"Mine, too. How about some hot tea and cold breakfast? It's the best I can do."

"Hot *tea*? For real?"

"Yes, tea, since you emphatically don't drink coffee." Hayley smirked as she produced a tall, narrow cook pot from her pack and poured water from the canteen into it. Then she set the pot on a rock she'd placed close to the blaze last night before turning in. "Shouldn't take long for the water to boil, but you surely don't need to consider tea a bribe for information."

"It's okay," Sean said gently. "You deserve to understand why I have recurring nightmares so you'll know it's not something going on inside me that will affect my attentiveness and capabilities while awake."

"Lots of people have nightmares that plague them and yet go about their lives just had bought them enough distance from their pursuers that the thugs wouldn't get within eyeshot of them before they all were forced to stop for the night.

Mack soon appeared, trotting along, tongue lolling. Sean sent him a glare the dog countered with a tail swish and an expression Sean could only describe as smug at chasing away the frightened moose.

About a mile later, another splotch of dense woodland swallowed them in stands of spruce, aspen, birch and pine. The trees cut the wind and rendered Sean marginally warmer. The relief was tempered by the necessity of a slower pace. His fingers—and his toes, too, since his socks had gotten wet—were in danger of frostbite. That fire couldn't happen soon enough.

"We're close now," Hayley said.

Sean pushed himself faster even as he forced his unfeeling fingers to ball and flex. He had to keep some circulation going. Why did he feel so tired? As if he wanted nothing more than to curl on the ground and let sleep take him? Sure, he'd gone overnight without sleep, but he'd skipped a night's rest before and not felt as if he could barely put one foot ahead of another. Creeping hypothermia.

Had to be. He couldn't allow the encroaching blackness in his mind to take him.

Had…to…keep…going.

Then they stepped out of the trees into a small clearing surrounded by woods. Sean blinked and forced himself to focus. The building sitting in the center of the open area barely deserved the name shack. The entire structure leaned in one direction and the porch had deteriorated so much it no longer connected to the cabin. One thing it had though, was a sturdy stone chimney, and a pile of chopped logs was stacked near it.

"Let's get inside." Hayley gripped his jacket, tugging him forward.

Sean took a step and stumbled. Standing still had been a mistake. His legs would barely function, and his body began to shudder.

"Get moving, mister!" Hayley's harsh shout echoed in his ears as if coming from a distance. "I can't carry you. You have to walk."

A sharp sting penetrated the numbness in Sean's cheek. He reared back, hauling in a deep breath. She'd slapped him.

*Good girl. Now, move, boy!*

Sean forced his wooden legs to move and his leaden feet to plod forward. With aching slowness, they crossed the yard, climbed onto the rickety porch and stepped through the door into the musty murk of the cabin's ancient interior.

On robotic feet, Sean allowed Hayley to lead him close to the cavernous hearth. The only thing missing was the one thing that could save him—a roaring blaze. But his brain couldn't seem to tell his body how to go about starting one. He was shutting down. Not good.

Hayley knelt and worked his boots off, then turned and dug through her pack. Sean swayed where he stood but couldn't figure out how to slump to the floor against the pressure of his frozen jeans around his legs.

"Get out of those wet pants and socks." Hayley's voice came to him as if from a distance. "And put these on. Do it now!"

Her bark galvanized him into sluggish action as she shoved a pair of dry long johns and socks at him. She turned away to rummage farther in her pack as Sean robotically complied with her order, the wet jeans snapping and crackling as he wrestled out of them. The long johns were a bit too small, but they hugged him with welcome warmth. Putting the socks on was beyond him, however.

Then Hayley turned and a large sheet enveloped his body. The Mylar blanket. Gentle hands urged him to a seat on the floor. Reality faded, and he drifted in a pale haze, not awake, but not unconscious either. Dimly, he registered brisk movement around him and someone putting the dry socks on his feet, but he no longer had the power to move. Gradually, blackness took him.

Warmth. Not the false warmth of advanced hypothermia, but genuine heat. Also, a crackling sound, and from somewhere near his nose, a crisp pine scent. The latter as much as anything had awakened him.

Sean opened his eyes and turned his head slightly. The movement brought a crinkling sound and a heightened pine odor. He was resting on evergreen boughs and covered with one of the Mylar blankets. Sean's gaze found the primary source of warmth—the fire dancing in the great hearth mere feet from his prone body.

Hayley! Where was she?

Sean raised himself on his elbows from the pine bed and spotted a form wrapped in a silvery Mylar blanket sitting at the far side of the hearth. Her injured leg was elevated on a chunk of firewood, the other one curled close to her body. Well, she wasn't really sitting. More like slumped, eyes closed, against the stone chimney surround, as if she'd been awake and keeping watch, but gradually slumber had gotten the better of her.

Mack lay near Hayley's feet, but at Sean's movement, the dog lifted his head. The animal seemed to grace Sean with a doggy grin and then resettled his great head onto his large paws and closed his eyes.

Sean also settled himself again. Hunger and thirst niggled at him but responding to those needs was too taxing. Weariness weighted his whole body and mind. Not surprising considering the exertions they'd undergone since he landed with Patterson's crooked crew at Hayley's homestead deep in the Alaskan bush.

After his mother died in the accident, and his father took him away to Portland to start work on a fishing boat, Sean had never thought to return to this part of the state. This was his mom's home stomping grounds where he'd spent his earliest childhood. Mom had been a constant then and his dad was around daily, rather than the arrangement in Portland of leaving Sean with his brother's family while he spent weeks and even months at sea.

Those early memories of Interior Alaska were vague, like faded and out-of-focus pictures. But they were overlaid with a sense of peace and contentment he'd never experienced since the day his childish antics triggered the greatest tragedy his life had ever known.

Sean shoved the searing memory away. As often as the terrifying recollection had swooped upon him—sometimes at the most inopportune moments—he should have learned by now there was no point in reliving the past. And no absolution either.

He gathered the Mylar blanket close to his neck and turned onto his side, facing away from the fire, and let the darkness claim him. But the refuge of sleep betrayed him, and the dream came. Horror swallowed him whole.

# EIGHT

A keening cry jerked Hayley awake. She sat up straight, and her stiff muscles complained at the sudden movement. Mack reared onto his haunches with a whine. They both stared at Sean, who thrashed on his bed of pine boughs, letting out wounded groans.

Was he ill? Did he have a fever?

Hayley scrambled forward on all fours and placed her hand against his forehead. The skin was warm but not unnaturally so.

At her touch, Sean lunged into a sitting position. His eyes popped wide, and a yelp exploded from his throat. Hayley scooted backward, and Mack stood on all fours with a bark that subsided into a soft growl. Hayley's heart pounded against her ribs.

Sean's chest heaved. Then he seemed to shake himself and the expression of vacant terror faded from his gaze. He blinked at her and Mack. Slowly, lucidity returned to his look.

His squared shoulders slumped, and he pinched the bridge of his nose with a thumb and forefinger. "I'm sorry. The last thing I wanted to do was wake you."

Hayley huffed. "I'd say the last thing you wanted to do was experience whatever dream was turning you inside out."

Sean's mouth quivered in what might have started to be a smile but turned into a frown. "Can't argue with you there." His tone was thin as a blade.

The wrenching sadness in his gaze twisted Hayley's insides. Mack padded forward and swiped his tongue against Sean's cheek. The man let out a shaky chuckle and ruffled the dog's fur. With an inexplicable lump in her throat, Hayley turned away and busied herself with feeding a few more logs onto the waning fire. Sean's dream had to have been about something intensely personal and painful.

She settled close to the blaze and drew her blanket around her shoulders, knees pulled close to her torso. The weathered old cabin didn't do well at holding the outdoor cold at bay. Occasional wind gusts infiltrated gaps in the wallboards and tousled the flames in the hearth, even as it nipped at exposed skin.

Hayley swiveled toward the ATF agent. He was looking at his watch. A waterproof variety, of course.

"It's almost five a.m.," he said. "Since we bedded down around the time the sun went down, we've actually had a decent night's sleep. But it won't get light out for hours yet, so we'll have to stay put for a while."

"I wonder how our pursuers are faring."

Sean smiled. "I doubt they're enjoying four walls around them—such as they are." He gazed around at their rough surroundings.

Hayley managed a light chuckle. "You don't adore the luxury accommodations?"

"Oh, I do." Sean grinned and the last of the nightmare shadows fled from his face. "I'd go so far as to call this fancy little shack a lifesaver…and you, too. Thank you. I would have been a goner without you."

His intense brown gaze burrowed warmth into her heart. She bit her lip against the impulse to ask about the dream that ended their night's rest. The question would be intrusive, wouldn't it? Then again, maybe there was something she should know about since they were fleeing for their lives together. Silence

fell as Hayley rearranged the burning logs
with a stick, sending sparks floating onto the
blackened hearthstones and urging the flames
to greater heights.

"I'll tell you," Sean said softly.

Hayley's jaw slackened. How did this guy
know she had a bad case of the curiosities?

"But I'd like a drink of water first," he said.
"My throat is dry as sandpaper."

"Mine, too. How about some hot tea and
cold breakfast? It's the best I can do."

"Hot *tea*? For real?"

"Yes, tea, since you emphatically don't
drink coffee." Hayley smirked as she produced a tall, narrow cook pot from her pack
and poured water from the canteen into it.
Then she set the pot on a rock she'd placed
close to the blaze last night before turning in.
"Shouldn't take long for the water to boil, but
you surely don't need to consider tea a bribe
for information."

"It's okay," Sean said gently. "You deserve
to understand why I have recurring nightmares so you'll know it's not something going
on inside me that will affect my attentiveness
and capabilities while awake."

"Lots of people have nightmares that
plague them and yet go about their lives just

fine." Not that she was about to let him know she was a member of that club. "But your dream must have been pretty intense."

"It always is." He frowned and stared into the dancing blaze.

"I can wait for a fireside chat until the tea is served."

He nodded without another word.

Hayley dumped water into a camp dish for Mack and fed him the last of the canine meal bars from the stash in her pack.

She rubbed the animal's soft flank as he ate and drank. "You'll have to hunt for yourself from now on, buddy."

He let out a muted *woof* as if he understood her words. Living in the Alaskan wilderness for half the year at a time had rendered the malamute a capable hunter, a survival skill many of his breed never needed to learn in civilized environments.

A few minutes later, Hayley handed Sean a mug of steaming liquid with a tea bag draped over the side. "No sweetener, I'm afraid."

"There's a limit to the luxury?" A smile flickered on his bearded face that was not reflected in his somber gaze. "This is great. Thanks." He took a sip and smacked his lips.

Hayley settled into a cross-legged pose and

nursed her tea. The nutty, faintly citrusy odor of the oolong was as comforting as the rich taste and warmth going down her throat. She said nothing further to Sean, oddly content to respect his choice whether or not to follow through with the explanation of his nightmare.

"Where to start?" Sean muttered. With his shuttered expression and soft tone, he seemed to be addressing himself, not her. Then his gaze lifted and snapped into focus on her face. "I killed my mother."

Hayley stiffened and choked on the tea halfway down her windpipe. "Wha-at?"

Sean's face went as red as the flames. "That didn't come out right. Sorry. That aspect of the car accident that killed her is always at the top of my mind so that bit slipped out first." He let out a long breath. "The years pass, but I've never stopped dreaming about that night. The collision. The shattering glass. The screams." His eyes slammed closed, and he visibly shuddered.

For leaden seconds, Hayley sat frozen. Then she lowered the tea mug from her face.

"This is what happened when you were seven?" The question came out thready, and she cleared her throat.

He nodded without meeting her gaze.

She leaned toward him. "How can a small child *cause* a car accident?"

He shrugged and took another sip of his tea, then laid the mug aside, his expression bleak. "It was the first time I'd been allowed to sit in the front passenger seat of the family car, and that was only because our back seat was filled with food and Christmas gifts for the local women's shelter. I was excited and fiddling with knobs and gadgets on the dash. Mom told me to quit, but it was like I couldn't help myself. She had a travel mug of hot coffee in the console, and somehow I managed to tip it onto her leg."

"So, she got distracted and hit something?"

"No." Sean shook his head like a dog shedding water. "Another driver ran a red light and hit *us* broadside."

"You've lost me." Hayley studied Sean's drawn face. "If another driver hit your vehicle, how was the accident your fault?"

"I shouldn't have been fooling around with the car gadgets."

"Agreed."

"I shouldn't have spilled coffee on my mother."

"Absolutely not, but—"

"Don't you get it?" Sean snarled. "If I hadn't distracted my mother, maybe she would have seen that other car and done something—anything—to avoid the wreck."

"And maybe—probably—the other vehicle would have struck yours anyway."

Sean gaped at her with his brows jammed together so tightly only a sliver of space remained between them. "It was my fault," he rasped. "He said it was."

"Who said?"

"My f-fath—" Sean seemed to choke over completing the word.

"Your father?" Heat scalded through Hayley's veins. Was the sensation mainly fury at Sean's dad or compassion for Sean? A turbulent cocktail of both, no doubt. She reached out and gripped Sean's shoulder. "That's ridiculous."

She stopped herself from blurting out cruel. How could a parent say such a horrible thing to their small child? Especially when the child has just lost his mother, and the father has just lost…his wife. The white heat inside her cooled to embers.

"Sounds like grief talking." Her tone had moderated. "How often has he said this to you?"

"Only the once. Right after it happened."

"And the statement stuck with you all these years."

"How could it not?"

"Maybe you should have a talk with your dad. It's possible he doesn't even remember saying those words. People blurt out all kinds of unfair and unkind things in the grip of grief. I should know."

Acid churned in Hayley's stomach. She should know indeed. Turning away, she grabbed the backpack and dug out the last of the beef jerky.

"Never mind me. I shouldn't be meddling. The psychology clinic has closed for the day." She held out a pair of strips toward Sean. "As advertised. Cold breakfast."

His dark gaze snared hers and held fast, even as he accepted the jerky from her fingers. Was he considering her suggestion to clear the air with his father? Or was he wondering what painful past she was hiding beneath those glib words, *I should know*, and the abrupt change of topic? How soon would it be her turn to bare unhealed wounds? Not soon, if she had anything to say about it. Not soon at all.

*Maybe it would be healthy if you did*, a

tiny voice, sounding strangely like her sister's, whispered in her heart.

Hayley closed her inner ears and chomped a bite out of her jerky.

In between bites of his breakfast, Sean sipped at the warm tea with determined concentration. What was the matter with him that he'd laid such a bombshell revelation on this woman he barely knew? Something about Hayley stripped away his defenses like no one else he'd ever met. Or was that impression only because they'd come together under such dangerous circumstances? She had proven herself a true and brave ally so perhaps he could be excused for trusting her deeply so quickly.

Her sharp response to his blurted revelation about his responsibility for his mother's death had shaken assumptions he'd harbored for over two decades. Those assumptions had long ground like grains of sand in his soul, slowly forming a protective callous in his heart that bore no resemblance to a beautiful pearl. The sense of being damaged goods had kept him a loner for a long time. His tough, independent mindset was part of what made him ideal as an undercover agent.

The few people he'd told of his sense of guilt—including the counselor he'd been assigned to see for mental health clearance before he went undercover—had responded with sympathetic platitudes designed to soothe rather than resolve. Not that he'd believed resolution possible, and he'd always figured others also saw the situation as irresolvable. At least, the counselor had signed off on his fitness for duty in the dangerous undercover realm. At the time, that was all that mattered to him.

But Hayley had skipped platitudes and jumped straight to confrontation. *Ridiculous*, she'd dubbed his assumption of guilt. Heat flared in Sean's belly. What did she know? She wasn't there when it happened. But then, she'd agreed he'd been misbehaving when the accident occurred. However, she didn't make the automatic leap between his bad actions and the car crash.

Absently, Sean chewed on the jerky, the salty savor strong on his tongue.

Sure, from his adult perspective, he mentally acknowledged the blame was not his alone. The other driver *had* run a red light. But ever since that day when his dad had verbally confirmed Sean's culpability in his mother's death, he'd never been able to shake off the conviction of fault. What if he *had* kept his hands to himself in the car that day? What if he *hadn't* knocked the coffee onto his mother? What if Mom had not been distracted? Would she still be alive?

He would never know the answer to the *what-ifs*. All he had was an acute awareness of what he'd done as a careless kid and that his father held him responsible. No wonder the man had gone off to sea more days of the year than he was home with his son.

But Hayley made all that reasoning sound bogus. Maybe his father hadn't meant what he said. Sean had never asked. Mostly because he couldn't bear to hear those words again from the lips of his only remaining parent. Maybe it was time for him to man up and have a difficult conversation with his father. But what if the rickety bridge that remained of his relationship with his dad couldn't bear the strain of the question?

"We need to make a plan and plot a course." Hayley's brisk words broke into Sean's bitter musings like a hatchet through ice.

Sean gave himself a mental shake. "Right." He rolled a crick out of his neck. "As badly as we need to acquire a sat phone, I'm not sure how we can use this cabin as a site to ambush our pursuers. There are too many of them. How likely is it that we can successfully outrun or evade the crooks on our trail?"

"That depends on how much farther we press on toward Nenana."

"Isn't reaching civilization our goal?"

Hayley shook her head. "Overland on foot, the journey would take weeks in the best of circumstances, and these aren't it. Serious winter will close in soon, and only a trained musher with significant supplies and a skilled dogsled team should even think about being out here."

"So, it's back to finding a way to call for help. We need the trooper's sat phone."

"Or Patterson's."

Sean snorted. "That guy is hunkered down in your cozy cabin, waiting for the grunts to deliver the goods—us. There's no doubt in my mind he was in the search plane that found us, and he and the pilot returned to base."

"What if we could get back to my homestead and retake the cabin?"

Sean finished the last of his tea and set the mug on the hearth with a dull clank. "That's a thought. We'd have to double back on our pursuers and sneak past them. Any ideas on how best to accomplish that feat?" He offered her a grin. "I've got faith in you, wilderness woman."

A blush spread across her cheeks as she returned his expectant gaze with steady brown eyes. What did she see when she looked at him? Disheveled and grimy, he must appear as rough as someone in a mountain man saga. But Hayley pulled off cute despite the hardships of the past days.

"Glenn's a sharp tracker," she said, "but I have a route in mind where we might be able to convince him we're serious about reaching Nenana—at least long enough for us to wheel around, creep past the criminal crew and make a break for home base. There, we'll only have to overcome two opponents—Patterson and the pilot. The drawback with that plan is even if we convince Glenn we're heading ever deeper into the bush, he'll eventually break off pursuit and take the crew back to the cabin himself."

"Because he'll know the wilderness will kill us without further effort on his part."

"Bingo. So, if we get around them, we'll have to travel fast to stay ahead—even faster than we've been going thus far."

Sean let out a low whistle through his teeth. "Then we'd better get on the move. Dawn is near enough to create a glow to travel by."

With a groan, he forced his aching body to a standing position. The wooden floor beneath his stocking feet was chilly. He glanced around and spotted his boots huddled in the shadows on the far side of the hearth, along with his jeans and socks.

Hayley laughed. "For a while there, after I got the fire going, your clothes were steaming like a clambake. They should be dry and toasty now."

Sean managed a grin as he grabbed the jeans and snugged them on over the long johns. Then he put on the boots. The footwear was warm through and through. "Once more, thank you from the bottom of my heart. How is your ankle today?"

"Better." She lifted a foot and swiveled it around. "I told you it wasn't a bad sprain. We should be able to make good time today. The morning leg of this journey will have us continuing to head northeast toward Nenana. Deeper into the bush. I'll be looking for promising terrain to hide our double-back from Glenn."

"If he picks up our trail after our waterway trick."

Hayley frowned. "He will. It's only a matter of time. How much time could spell the difference between success or failure of our little ploy."

"Got it." Sean jerked a nod. "Before we get too far, we'll need a water source." He gestured toward the canteen sitting by the backpack. "There can't be much left in there after high tea this morning."

"No worries," Hayley said, stooping to stuff their Mylar blankets into the mouth of the pack. "There's a spring behind the cabin. One of the reasons this structure was built here. But eventually, a water source wasn't enough motivation for anyone to linger in such a remote spot. Thus, the cabin was abandoned."

"How are we fixed for food?"

She frowned and shook her head. "I have a couple of MREs for us at lunch. We'll need the calories."

Sean chuckled. "Meals ready to eat? I suppose the military isn't the only source for those these days."

Hayley turned her attention to the fire and began to poke at it with a stick, separating the smoldering remnants of logs so they could no longer feed off each other and would soon burn out. "MREs are readily available in wilderness outfitter stores. I've also got a good-sized bag of pine nuts my brother and I dried over the summer, but that's about it. We'll have to forage for supper."

"How much forage is available this late in the year?"

She smirked, hefted the pack and led the way toward the door. "Won't you be surprised. Your taste buds will be, anyway."

"I can hardly wait." His tone was dry.

She let out a low chuckle as she pulled wide the door and admitted a whoosh of cold air that scoured Sean's cheeks. The darkness outside had only begun to pale toward a grim dawn. The day ahead did not beckon; it threatened.

Hardening his jaw, Sean slung the Winchester rifle and the automatic rifle over opposite shoulders. Then he tromped after Hayley as he pulled on his warm and dry gloves and hat. A handgun would have been a nice addition to their armament, as well as more ammunition for the guns in their possession, but wishing didn't get them anything. Hopefully, Patterson's crew were also feeling the pinch of low ammo.

As he stepped out the door, a gust of wind stole his breath. He hunched deeper into his jacket as Hayley led them around to the back of the structure. She must be heading for that spring she mentioned. They placed their feet carefully in the predawn dimness. A few feet into the trees, they met a lichen-covered wall of rock. Skirting the low cliff face, Sean followed his guide over and around tumbled boulders. A gentle tinkle of water soon met his ears.

Then they came in sight of the water's source emerging in little more than a slow trickle from a crack in the cliff face a few feet off the ground. A small pool of liquid gathered in a rocky hollow, while the rest of the stream crept onward obliquely in a narrow but gradually widening path that sported a thin sheen of ice.

Hayley pointed in the direction the water led. "There's another marsh occupying a low spot in the terrain over there, but we'll only be skirting it." She knelt and began filling the canteen.

"I'm happy to avoid any marshes, but I'm a little nervous about the lower temperature today."

"Me, too." She rose, screwing the cover on the canteen. "The heavy air feels like a storm brewing, and it's likely to be snow, not rain. And in this wind—" She shook her head without finishing the sentence.

Sean got the picture. Their horrible situation would become exponentially more dangerous if a blizzard struck. That the circumstance would be equally dire for their pursuers offered marginal comfort. The status of hunter and hunted would mean nothing if they all froze to death.

*God, please help us.*

Sean inhaled a sharp breath. What was up with the brief prayers he'd been spurting since he'd met Hayley? He and God hadn't been on speaking terms much since his mom's passing. She'd always brought him faithfully to church, but his father's family weren't churchgoers, and his own attendance had fallen by the wayside. If they survive this mess, maybe it was time to rethink his neglect of faith.

# NINE

Hayley led her little troop along the edge of the marshy ground and soon found what she'd been looking for—a significant stand of cattails. She reached over and pulled one out of the ground and studied the root.

"Looks good and healthy." She sent a glance toward Sean, who was standing, hands on hips, with his eyebrows raised.

"Good for what?"

She waggled the root at him. "You're looking at supper."

Sean scowled. "Don't tell me it's going to taste like chicken."

Hayley laughed. "No, more like potatoes. Give me a hand. There are a couple of forage bags in the pack. We'll put about a dozen roots in one bag and the heads—the cattail part—in another bag."

"We can eat the heads, too?"

"Nope, but they make excellent fire starters. If it were spring, we could harvest and eat the pollen and the shoots. The stalks would also be tender and edible."

Sean rolled his shoulders and dug out the forage bags. "You're the expert. I'll have to trust you."

"Good choice." She showed him how to peel the fibrous outer coating from each root before placing it in the bag. "If we wait until the root dries to peel away the excess fiber, the chore becomes extra difficult. It's best to take the time to do it now."

They finished their task, stored their harvest and moved on. Hayley led them along a path skirting the marsh but on dry ground. After a mile of leaving decent tracks in the soft turf, they came to a rockier area and she turned away from the marsh to follow a terrain less apt to leave traces of their passage. Mack crisscrossed from side to side or ahead or behind them, sometimes sniffing the ground, other times scenting the air. Occasionally, he darted off into the trees but always came back into sight within a few minutes.

About midmorning, a snowflake brushed a cool finger across Hayley's forehead, and she frowned up at the sullen sky. "We won't be able to hide our tracks if we get a modest accumulation of white stuff. Unless the snowfall turns into a track-obliterating blizzard, but that would be even worse."

"How about we pick up the pace?"

"You game?"

She glanced toward her companion, who had been silent for most of the morning. Sean nodded without speaking and broke into a low trot with her.

Was he feeling uncomfortable about sharing personal details at the cabin? She'd like to tell him not to worry; she wasn't one to expose other people's problems. She barely even talked about her own. But she didn't want to bring up a painful subject with Sean again in case she was reading him wrong. And she certainly didn't want to open herself to a tit for tat on her own painful unresolved losses.

When Hayley's engagement went up in flames as a result of her sister Kirsten's death, there had been plenty of blame to assign. Yet the conversation with Sean this morning had pricked her heart. Had she been as unfair and unkind as Sean's father in assigning blame?

No. She firmed her jaw. Ryan hadn't pulled the trigger, but his obsession with his job had put both Kirsten and her in harm's way—and Kirsten had paid the ultimate price. Years had passed, and she still hadn't learned how to forgive the man. Nor had she found another romantic relationship to replace the one she'd lost. Maybe her inability to forgive was the reason she was alone. Did she have the guts to consider that possibility?

Not at this moment when they were evading bullets and bad guys, not to mention hungry four-legged predators. And now with the drop in temperature, the lowering clouds and moisture gathering in the air—harbingers of an early snowstorm—the weather was starting to conspire against them, too. She needed her wits about her. But, for the moment, they needed to halt and take a breather. Her ankle was beginning to bother her again.

At her suggestion, Sean and she settled down on a low, flat rock. Hayley gobbled down a few painkillers and analgesics, then passed out handfuls of pine nuts. Nose to the ground, Mack sneaked off into the trees and disappeared from view.

"So, tell me about your family," Sean said. "You have a brother that you've mentioned, and your parents live in Texas. Any other siblings?"

Hayley's gut clenched, and she shot a sidelong glance at her companion. He wasn't even looking at her as his gaze continually scanned their surroundings. Good situational awareness, as she'd noticed before. Clearly, he was only attempting light, normal conversation. Hayley willed her muscles to relax. Though this was not a conversation she wanted to have, a defensive response would only grab his attention and invite more questions.

"I had a twin sister." Her attempt at calmness resulted in a deadpan tone.

"Had?" Sean's gaze met hers, and his eyes widened.

Hayley huffed out a long breath, steaming the air. "Kirsten was killed a little over eight years ago on our twenty-first birthday."

"Wow! I'm so sorry."

Of all the times Hayley had heard those words from people's mouths, this was the first time the genuine compassion pulsed strongly enough to resonate in her heart. Maybe Sean's expression of sympathy crept past her defenses because he'd bared his own profound pain to her mere hours ago. Whatever the reason, the sincerity of his apology for her loss spread a balm like warm honey through her insides.

"Do you want to talk about it?" His tone was gentle.

Hayley shook her head. "No."

Sean said nothing more, but his hand wrapped around hers. With the pressure, the wounds on the back of her hand stung faintly, but she didn't care. The gesture was welcome.

Mack trotted into the small clearing, his nose up, sniffing at the air. Hayley rose, and Sean beside her. She gazed around, but nothing appeared out of the ordinary in their immediate area and no telltale buzz told of an approaching aircraft.

Sean grabbed the binoculars from the pack and stood atop their log, scanning the area. "Look!"

He handed her the binoculars, and she joined him standing on the log. She focused the lenses back in the direction from which they had come. Now that daylight had fully come, it was possible to see the trail of dark smoke that snaked upward into the leaden sky.

"Did an ember escape the fireplace and start the cabin on fire?" Sean asked.

"Possible, but not likely. I placed the still-smoldering logs where the wind through the chinks in the walls would be least likely to reach the embers and carry a spark."

"Then the other possibility would be—"

"Our pursuers are there and hunkering down in front of the fireplace to ride out the coming storm."

"Exactly." Sean nodded, wide-eyed like she'd taken the words straight out of his mouth.

Hayley smirked to herself. They were still finishing each other's sentences like two souls of the same mind. Almost like Kirsten and she used to do.

Sean frowned. "Which leaves us out in the cold."

"Which leaves us with a golden opportunity to double back toward my homestead. The traces of our presence at the cabin will assure Glenn he's on our trail. I doubt he'll consider us doubling back. Let's hurry. We'll make what progress we can before the snow comes in earnest." With her words, a snowflake drifted down and landed wet and cold on the end of her nose.

Hayley led them at right angles to their former direction. The terrain remained relatively flat and sparsely wooded so they were able to hold to a steady, slow trot. Flakes fell with increasing frequency, muting sight and scent as if the world were closing in around them.

No, he'd be wise not to indulge false hopes. [Se]an suppressed a sigh. If—when—they got [o]ut of this situation, Hayley and he would no [d]oubt be going their separate ways.

He'd also have quite an after-action report [t]o fill out, explaining how a civilian had become so integral to fulfilling his assignment. He didn't know how he would have stopped the sale of the weapon without her, and she was key to their wilderness survival now. Frankly, she was the hero of the story. She might get some sort of citizen commendation.

An hour then two crept by with the snowfall swirling in front of their little hut's opening. Judging by the limpness of her body and the steady depth of her breathing, Hayley must have dozed off. Sean didn't blame her. She probably hadn't slept much last night, what with watching over him and keeping [t]he fire going.

At last, the snowfall began to wane and [th]e howl of the wind diminished. Should he [a]waken Hayley? They should get on the move [o]n. Sean's stomach growled. Maybe they [c]ould eat first. Their light breakfast and pine [nu]t snack were long digested.

[A]bruptly, Mack's head lifted from his [pa]ws, his ears perked up and his nostrils

Two miles passed beneath their feet and then Hayley called a halt. The wind was picking up and the snow was intensifying.

"Before we're slogging through a blizzard and can't see a thing, we have to build a shelter."

"Tell me what to do." Sean nodded. His beard poking from his tightly tied jacket hood wore a frosting of white.

"We'll start with that deadfall over there." She pointed toward a spot where a pine tree had collapsed at an angle against a live aspen. "We'll chop off the dead branches and twigs beneath the trunk, creating a space beneath. Then we'll gather or chop branches to lean up against the trunk to form walls. Gobs of dirt and leaves will seal the cracks. The shelter should be less drafty than that old cabin. Our body heat huddled together is what will keep us warm."

"No fire, then?" Sean began grabbing up long sticks and placing them in a pile.

Hayley retrieved her hunting knife and small hatchet from her pack. "Not a good idea when your tiny shelter is cobbled together from dry, flammable material. If we could place the fire at least a few feet distant from our makeshift hut, I might consider it, but it won't stay lit in this snow and wind."

Twenty minutes later, the leaf and stick hut had taken shape. The snow and wind had also intensified to the point that visibility drew near zero. At least she guesstimated the temperature to remain in the upper twenties. If this were December or later, they'd be looking at the kind of single-digit or below-zero temps that would make a fire mandatory, despite the difficulties and risks.

"Let's g-get inside," Hayley called to Sean between chattering teeth.

She shoved him toward the opening and followed him into the dark interior. At Hayley's instigation, the two humans crowded into the shelter against the back wall farthest from the opening. They wrapped Mylar blankets around themselves, and the dog curled up close to them, blocking any intrusion of snow or wind with his bulk. The cessation of cold wind and colder snow brought immediate relief to Hayley's shivering body.

As Sean wrapped his sturdy arms around her and drew her close, Hayley didn't resist. Closeness was necessary. And as much as she'd love to deny it, snuggling with this ATF agent she'd barely met felt anything but alien and uncomfortable. Apparently, danger bred intimacy...or could there be another factor?

Would she find herself this attract under more normal conditions? V ever be given the opportunity to fi

They were in treacherous circums every way. Survival was far from gua Yet if she could choose to be elsewhere having met this extraordinary man who his mission to save her, would she do so shocking to realize she might not take th tion. Was ATF Special Agent Sean O'K worth crossing *lawman* off her no-date Even considering the notion was the most sonally earthshaking question of all.

In the close darkness, Sean kept his wrapped firmly but gently around Ha shoulders. She leaned into him with he against his chest. The compact spa growing steadily warmer, their bo effectively combating the wintry cl shivers subsided, as did his, and th piney aroma of the shelter teased hi

When was the last time he'd snu anyone, much less a lovely woma and courage? Not that her embrace thing other than the practicalities the storm, but a guy could preter someone who wanted to be clos flared. Sean went stiff. What did the dog hear and smell? Surely, their pursuers couldn't have caught up with them. For one thing, it would have been foolish for them to leave the cabin and travel during the storm. For another, Hayley and his tracks would have been obliterated by the snow, so Trooper Glenn would have had no trail to follow.

"What is it?" Hayley murmured, sitting up straight and leaving the shelter of his arms.

"Mack hears or smells something."

Hayley leaned forward and laid a hand on her dog's back. "What is it, boy?"

Snapping, popping sounds carried faintly in the wintry stillness.

"Something large is approaching through the trees," Sean murmured.

"A bunch of large somethings."

Sean's gut twisted. Maybe he was wrong about their pursuers catching up with them. Schooling his breathing, he pulled his automatic weapon forward. A guttural chuffing began to accompany the snapping of dry branches. Hayley reached out and pressed the gun muzzle downward, and Sean did not resist. Whatever approached wasn't human— not making those kinds of sounds.

"Some kind of deer?" he whispered.

"Caribou, I think." Her voice was hardly louder than a breath. "As winter approaches, they leave the mountains and drift into the boreal forest. Stay still, and let's watch them pass." She followed her words to Sean with a soft command for Mack to remain quiet.

In tandem with Hayley, Sean scooted to the mouth of their shelter. A minute later, a large brown animal with a white neck, chest, and rump plodded into full view and stopped. Lifting its head high, its broad nostrils quivered as the bull caribou scented the air. The majestic antlers on the creature's crown were not flat like a moose's antlers, but rounded and tall and shaped like a curve with many prongs. A few icicles dangling from the tips enhanced the spiky look. In the bull's wake, at least a dozen smaller female caribou with more modest antlers also halted, their bodies partly blocked by trees. The huffing breaths of the herd fogged the air, and a musty odor filled the clearing.

How many people ever got to see these beasts up close like this in the wild? An odd sensation quivered through Sean. Exuberance? Exultation? Considering the urban location in which he'd spent most of his childhood and all his adult life, this environment should feel alien to him, but it didn't. He liked it. A lot. If not for the dangerous gang pursuing them, he'd be having the time of his life.

Mack quivered and whined. The sound of a potential predator spurred the caribou into flight. Snow flew and hooves thumped. As kicked-up spritzes of white sprayed his face, Sean let out the laugh he'd been suppressing.

Hayley punched him in the arm. "You do know the herd could have charged right through our rigged-up shelter and not lost a step."

Sean grinned down at her. "This experience is bringing back early memories to me of my uncles taking me trekking and hunting in the bush. I've forgotten nearly everything I learned from them, but I feel like...like this man-child is finally home. Once we get free of this mess, I'm definitely coming back here to explore, whether or not my mother's people welcome me."

"Your mother's people?"

"She was three-quarters Athabaskan."

"I've been wondering if you had indigenous blood. Why wouldn't they welcome you?"

"Because my dad said they didn't want to see us anymore after..." His voice trailed away as an invisible fist squeezed his windpipe.

"You assumed they also blamed you for your mother's death. Did your dad say that was the reason?"

"Not in so many words."

Hayley sniffed. "I'm skeptical, but if that's the truth, they only have themselves to blame for missing out on knowing you."

Sean's chest warmed. "Thank you." His throat was so full he could hardly say the words. He'd never received a higher compliment.

"We should eat our MREs and then take advantage of this stellar opportunity."

"Opportunity?" He jerked his attention back onto the practicalities of their situation.

"The caribou have churned up the snow into a mass of sloppy prints, and the herd is going in the right direction for us. We're going to follow them as long as they're headed the way we need to go and hope their tracks will render ours less noticeable to the low-lifes hunting us."

"Sounds like a plan."

Twenty minutes later, they left their shelter, bellies full of goop that tasted like food out of a can, but the taste was a secondary consideration to the high calories the meal provided. Sean stretched his arms and inhaled deeply

Two miles passed beneath their feet and then Hayley called a halt. The wind was picking up and the snow was intensifying.

"Before we're slogging through a blizzard and can't see a thing, we have to build a shelter."

"Tell me what to do." Sean nodded. His beard poking from his tightly tied jacket hood wore a frosting of white.

"We'll start with that deadfall over there." She pointed toward a spot where a pine tree had collapsed at an angle against a live aspen. "We'll chop off the dead branches and twigs beneath the trunk, creating a space beneath. Then we'll gather or chop branches to lean up against the trunk to form walls. Gobs of dirt and leaves will seal the cracks. The shelter should be less drafty than that old cabin. Our body heat huddled together is what will keep us warm."

"No fire, then?" Sean began grabbing up long sticks and placing them in a pile.

Hayley retrieved her hunting knife and small hatchet from her pack. "Not a good idea when your tiny shelter is cobbled together from dry, flammable material. If we could place the fire at least a few feet distant from our makeshift hut, I might consider it, but it won't stay lit in this snow and wind."

Twenty minutes later, the leaf and stick hut had taken shape. The snow and wind had also intensified to the point that visibility drew near zero. At least she guesstimated the temperature to remain in the upper twenties. If this were December or later, they'd be looking at the kind of single-digit or below-zero temps that would make a fire mandatory, despite the difficulties and risks.

"Let's g-get inside," Hayley called to Sean between chattering teeth.

She shoved him toward the opening and followed him into the dark interior. At Hayley's instigation, the two humans crowded into the shelter against the back wall farthest from the opening. They wrapped Mylar blankets around themselves, and the dog curled up close to them, blocking any intrusion of snow or wind with his bulk. The cessation of cold wind and colder snow brought immediate relief to Hayley's shivering body.

As Sean wrapped his sturdy arms around her and drew her close, Hayley didn't resist. Closeness was necessary. And as much as she'd love to deny it, snuggling with this ATF agent she'd barely met felt anything but alien and uncomfortable. Apparently, danger bred intimacy…or could there be another factor?

Would she find herself this attracted to Sean under more normal conditions? Would she ever be given the opportunity to find out?

They were in treacherous circumstances in every way. Survival was far from guaranteed. Yet if she could choose to be elsewhere, never having met this extraordinary man who risked his mission to save her, would she do so? How shocking to realize she might not take that option. Was ATF Special Agent Sean O'Keefe worth crossing *lawman* off her no-date list? Even considering the notion was the most personally earthshaking question of all.

In the close darkness, Sean kept his arms wrapped firmly but gently around Hayley's shoulders. She leaned into him with her head against his chest. The compact space was growing steadily warmer, their body heat effectively combating the wintry chill. Her shivers subsided, as did his, and the earthy, piney aroma of the shelter teased his nostrils.

When was the last time he'd snuggled with anyone, much less a lovely woman of grace and courage? Not that her embrace meant anything other than the practicalities of surviving the storm, but a guy could pretend he'd found someone who wanted to be close to him.

No, he'd be wise not to indulge false hopes. Sean suppressed a sigh. If—when—they got out of this situation, Hayley and he would no doubt be going their separate ways.

He'd also have quite an after-action report to fill out, explaining how a civilian had become so integral to fulfilling his assignment. He didn't know how he would have stopped the sale of the weapon without her, and she was key to their wilderness survival now. Frankly, she was the hero of the story. She might get some sort of citizen commendation.

An hour then two crept by with the snowfall swirling in front of their little hut's opening. Judging by the limpness of her body and the steady depth of her breathing, Hayley must have dozed off. Sean didn't blame her. She probably hadn't slept much last night, what with watching over him and keeping the fire going.

At last, the snowfall began to wane and the howl of the wind diminished. Should he awaken Hayley? They should get on the move soon. Sean's stomach growled. Maybe they should eat first. Their light breakfast and pine nut snack were long digested.

Abruptly, Mack's head lifted from his paws, his ears perked up and his nostrils flared. Sean went stiff. What did the dog hear and smell? Surely, their pursuers couldn't have caught up with them. For one thing, it would have been foolish for them to leave the cabin and travel during the storm. For another, Hayley and his tracks would have been obliterated by the snow, so Trooper Glenn would have had no trail to follow.

"What is it?" Hayley murmured, sitting up straight and leaving the shelter of his arms.

"Mack hears or smells something."

Hayley leaned forward and laid a hand on her dog's back. "What is it, boy?"

Snapping, popping sounds carried faintly in the wintry stillness.

"Something large is approaching through the trees," Sean murmured.

"A bunch of large somethings."

Sean's gut twisted. Maybe he was wrong about their pursuers catching up with them. Schooling his breathing, he pulled his automatic weapon forward. A guttural chuffing began to accompany the snapping of dry branches. Hayley reached out and pressed the gun muzzle downward, and Sean did not resist. Whatever approached wasn't human—not making those kinds of sounds.

"Some kind of deer?" he whispered.

"Caribou, I think." Her voice was hardly louder than a breath. "As winter approaches, they leave the mountains and drift into the boreal forest. Stay still, and let's watch them pass." She followed her words to Sean with a soft command for Mack to remain quiet.

In tandem with Hayley, Sean scooted to the mouth of their shelter. A minute later, a large brown animal with a white neck, chest, and rump plodded into full view and stopped. Lifting its head high, its broad nostrils quivered as the bull caribou scented the air. The majestic antlers on the creature's crown were not flat like a moose's antlers, but rounded and tall and shaped like a curve with many prongs. A few icicles dangling from the tips enhanced the spiky look. In the bull's wake, at least a dozen smaller female caribou with more modest antlers also halted, their bodies partly blocked by trees. The huffing breaths of the herd fogged the air, and a musty odor filled the clearing.

How many people ever got to see these beasts up close like this in the wild? An odd sensation quivered through Sean. Exuberance? Exultation? Considering the urban location in which he'd spent most of his childhood and all his adult life, this environment should feel alien to him, but it didn't. He liked it. A lot. If not for the dangerous gang pursuing them, he'd be having the time of his life.

Mack quivered and whined. The sound of a potential predator spurred the caribou into flight. Snow flew and hooves thumped. As kicked-up spritzes of white sprayed his face, Sean let out the laugh he'd been suppressing.

Hayley punched him in the arm. "You do know the herd could have charged right through our rigged-up shelter and not lost a step."

Sean grinned down at her. "This experience is bringing back early memories to me of my uncles taking me trekking and hunting in the bush. I've forgotten nearly everything I learned from them, but I feel like...like this man-child is finally home. Once we get free of this mess, I'm definitely coming back here to explore, whether or not my mother's people welcome me."

"Your mother's people?"

"She was three-quarters Athabaskan."

"I've been wondering if you had indigenous blood. Why wouldn't they welcome you?"

"Because my dad said they didn't want to see us anymore after..." His voice trailed away as an invisible fist squeezed his windpipe.

"You assumed they also blamed you for your mother's death. Did your dad say that was the reason?"

"Not in so many words."

Hayley sniffed. "I'm skeptical, but if that's the truth, they only have themselves to blame for missing out on knowing you."

Sean's chest warmed. "Thank you." His throat was so full he could hardly say the words. He'd never received a higher compliment.

"We should eat our MREs and then take advantage of this stellar opportunity."

"Opportunity?" He jerked his attention back onto the practicalities of their situation.

"The caribou have churned up the snow into a mass of sloppy prints, and the herd is going in the right direction for us. We're going to follow them as long as they're headed the way we need to go and hope their tracks will render ours less noticeable to the lowlifes hunting us."

"Sounds like a plan."

Twenty minutes later, they left their shelter, bellies full of goop that tasted like food out of a can, but the taste was a secondary consideration to the high calories the meal provided. Sean stretched his arms and inhaled deeply of the wet powder's fresh scent. Around eight inches of snow coated the ground, reaching nearly to the top of his boots.

Hayley mimicked his stretching actions. "The air is warming. This early in the season, most of the snow will melt before bitter weather closes in to stay." She reached a hand toward him. "Let me have my rifle. I'll let you carry the pack and the automatic."

Sean complied, and Hayley began to move out.

"Remember to keep your footfalls within the churned path of the herd," she said with a glance over her shoulder.

Sean followed her lithe figure. "Our tracks don't look anything like the double half-moons of the caribou."

"That's why, if our pursuers catch up to us, the best we can expect is for this ploy to confuse Glenn for a time, not throw him off entirely."

"I'm all for making things harder for the crooks. But maybe the trooper traitor has lost us entirely after the cabin. The snow obliterated our tracks back there. They might not find our trail."

"In that case, they're going to return to the homestead—"

"Just like we are." Sean let out a low groan. "Can't be helped."

"We need speed now more than ever."

"Let's burn some calories."

Her grin set Sean's heart tripping over itself. He matched her trotting pace while Mack bounded in circles around them, giddy in the snow. Moving along with the path already trampled by the herd minimized the suction of the wet powder against their boots, allowing them to make swift progress.

In less than an hour, the trees grew sparse as they entered an open plain sloping gently toward a small lake. Hayley halted at the edge of a stand of golden larch trees, and Sean stopped beside her, intending to catch his breath but losing it to the view. The intensely blue water shimmered diamond-like under a thin sheen of clear ice. The caribou herd had stopped at the edge of the lake and were milling gently, stomping through the ice coating and refreshing themselves with the water.

Mack charged ahead, barking. The caribou spooked and tore off at an oblique angle toward the nearest tree cover. Hayley called to her dog, and Mack whirled away from his pursuit. He returned toward them, head high in a jaunty trot like he'd won an award.

Sean laughed, and Hayley joined him.

What he wouldn't give for a video camera about now—that and no bloodthirsty crooks on their trail. At the mental reminder, Sean glanced over his shoulder to check what marks their running pace had left in the herd trail.

"What do you notice?" Hayley asked.

"Our higher pace lengthened our stride, and our feet spent minimal time in contact with the ground, which makes our human tracks less discernible in the snow and mud mix caused by the herd's hooves."

Hayley laughed. "You'll morph into an outdoorsman yet. And as the snow continues to melt, our tracks will become even less evident."

Sean gazed into her sparkling dark eyes. Her cheeks were ruddy from the chill, and tendrils of her tawny hair peeked out from the fur lining of the parka hood that framed her strong yet fine-boned features.

"Beautiful." The word at the tip of Sean's thoughts escaped his lips.

The smile left her eyes, and she turned away. "Don't. I can't like you. Not like that."

Back rigid, she moved down the slope toward the water. "We'll fill the canteen, then move on toward the homestead, taking a different route than the herd."

Sean stomped in her wake. "I'm not going to apologize because I find you attractive."

Hayley didn't respond except to increase her pace.

Sean caught up to her at the edge of the water where she had knelt to fill the canteen. "I'm not expecting anything from you except an explanation. What do you mean you *can't* like me? Because of the things I told you about myself?"

Hayley stood and whirled toward him. "Of course not. The problem is me, not you. And that's not a cliché in this case. It's true."

Gut twisting, Sean glared into her somber eyes.

She turned her whitened face away, biting her lower lip. At last, she let out a sigh. "Okay, I'll tell you about my ex-fiancé and what happened to my sister. Maybe then you'll understand."

Sean's heart hammered against his ribs. Hayley had been engaged? And how had her ex been involved in the sister's death? Was it terrible of him to need to know the answers to those questions? Hayley opened her mouth, and Sean nearly held his breath to catch every word of what she was about to say.

Mack's throaty bark shattered the moment.

They both whirled toward the dog. The animal's nose was pointed skyward as his frenzied barking continued.

"Oh, no!" Hayley pointed a finger toward a distant object winging toward them in the sky. "Glenn lost us, so he must have called the boss for an aerial search, and—"

"Now Patterson has found us."

Sean's teeth ground together. Whatever Hayley had been about to tell him might not matter now or forever if they wound up dead in the snow.

# TEN

"We'll never reach cover before we're spotted," Hayley said. "But we need to make a break for the trees anyway."

She darted toward the forest. Sean's footfalls hammered at her heels. Mack remained behind them, barking and growling as if he could hold the plane at bay by sheer ferocity.

The circumstances of Sean's tragic loss of his mother at a tender age kept him emotionally isolated to this day. What did that reveal about her alone status and the health of her own emotions when she'd almost prefer running for her life over baring her still-raw anguish to another human soul?

At least, at this moment, they didn't have to worry about being shot at. That could wait until Glenn's hunters caught up with them.

"Faster!" Sean's shout rang inches from her ear.

The buzz of the plane grew almost deafening. Hayley risked a look over her shoulder, and her pulse rate rocketed. What was it that she'd been thinking about no one shooting at them? How wrong could she be?

The aircraft loomed large and all too close as someone poked the dark barrel of a weapon out the passenger window. Her imagination drew a manic grin on the face of the man about to rain bullets on them.

Suddenly, Sean halted, got down on one knee and raised his automatic weapon.

"Go, go, go!" he shouted urgently. "You and Mack get out of here. Somebody has to survive."

Hayley stumbled, and her healing ankle protested the awkward movement. She started to lift her rifle, but Mack's powerful jaws clamped onto her jacket, whirling her around and dragging her onward toward the tree line.

A cacophony of gunfire rent the air, lending wings to Hayley's feet. Her pulse throbbed in her neck and her heart hammered against her ribs. If she looked over her shoulder, what would she see? Sean's body sprawled in reddening snow?

*Please, God, let him survive.*

A second spate of gunfire roared, and the timbre of the plane's engine changed.

Hayley reached the trees, slid to a halt in the slick powder and turned around, every muscle in her body drawn tense as bowstrings. The breath heaved in her lungs as her gaze sought out Sean. There he was, still kneeling, gun raised.

*Thank You, Jesus.*

The aircraft had pulled up and was turning away from them, a slight sputter in its progress. As the plane began to grow smaller, a tendril of smoke spurted in its wake. Hayley grinned. *So, there, bad guys.* A cheer left her lips. The ATF agent had clipped their bird's wings, figuratively speaking.

She returned her gaze to Sean, who had pulled himself into a standing position. He turned and took a few steps in her direction, then stumbled and fell on his face.

"Sean!" Her feet flew over the ground toward him.

By the time she reached him, he was stirring and groaning. Not dead. Hayley hauled in a deep breath. Shaking, she fell to her knees beside him as he struggled to rise.

"Whoa! You're hit," she said, pressing him back down to earth.

His face had gone paper pale. "Took one in the left side." He huffed between gritted teeth. "I think—hope—it's a graze or a shallow through-and-though."

She examined the left side of his jacket, which sported a telltale hole, front and back, but it was impossible to see how much damage had been done to his flesh. However, the wetness soaking through the fabric wasn't a good sign.

Hayley frowned. "We need to stop the bleeding."

"Let's make tree cover first." He began getting to his feet, uttering deep groans.

She had no choice but to lend her arm for assistance, though she was far from sure standing up and moving around was the best behavior right now. "The bad guys won't be coming back. You damaged their plane."

"I don't care to take that chance." Sean stood upright, swaying.

"I'm taking the pack."

Hayley stripped the heavy item from his back, then turned and offered him her shoulder to lean on. Mack trotted up to them, whining softly. She held the pack strap toward him, and his jaws gripped the canvas.

"Go, boy." She motioned him to go ahead of them.

The dog dragged the pack across the snow

as they all made their way into the forest.
About ten paces in, Sean stopped. He let out
a moan as Hayley helped him lower himself
to the ground and lean against a birch trunk.

"Can you get your jacket open?" she asked.

Without a word, Sean pulled down the
zipper and spread the outer garment wide.
Hayley sucked in a sharp breath. Blood had
soaked one side of his checked, flannel shirt.
The tip of her tongue poking out between her
teeth, she lifted the shirt and peered closely at
the wound. It wasn't gushing blood, at least
not anymore, but it was oozing steadily.

"A graze," she pronounced. "But it's deep
and long. I think a rib deflected the bullet."

Sean let out a grunt. "No wonder it hurts
to breathe. The rib may be broken."

"We need to stop the bleeding and disinfect the gash."

Hayley hurriedly dug in her pack for the
trauma kit. She pulled out a strip of hemo-
static gauze and pressed it firmly against the
wound. Sean inhaled a sharp breath but didn't
flinch or complain as they waited several
minutes to give the clotting process time to
begin. At last, Hayley eased the gauze away
from the area and inspected it.

"Good. The bleeding is arrested, and the

wound looks clean. This is going to sting," she said as she took disinfectant pads from their sealed packets.

The process of applying the pads and wrapping his torso firmly with cloth bandages took several minutes of soft groans and huffs from Sean and gentle clucks from Hayley. Then she sat back on her haunches and surveyed her handiwork.

"I'd love to get you to a hospital ASAP. You need stitches. But until that becomes possible, this will have to do."

"You did great." He offered a strained smile. "Thank you."

"No. Thank *you*." Hayley blinked her eyes rapidly against the sting of tears. "You risked your life for Mack and me."

A trace of color crept onto his cheeks. "The least I can do when you're a total innocent caught up in trouble, not of your making."

"Not. Your. Fault." She pronounced each word with emphasis. "I would be dead now without your presence. Mack, too, probably."

Their gazes locked, and the breath vacated Hayley's lungs. What exactly was this yearning feeling deep within when she looked at Sean? Gratitude? Yes, but not merely that. It was the something else that scared the skittish part of her that had so long guarded her heart.

Sean broke eye contact with her and stirred. "We should get going."

"No." Hayley shook her head. "You need to rest, hydrate and eat—at least for the next twenty minutes to a half hour."

"Twenty minutes. No longer." He shook a finger at her. "Glenn's crew will have our co-ordinates now."

"Then, the more reason you'll need your strength."

"Agreed." His expression relaxed into a smile.

Hayley handed Sean the canteen and some of the painkiller and analgesic tablets she'd been taking for her ankle. Then she pulled out the bag of pine nuts. Sean accepted her offerings with soft words of thanks. With him settled, she allowed herself to sit opposite him with her back against a tree trunk. Mack huffed at the humans snacking without him, turned and trotted off into the trees.

"While we regroup," she said, "and Mack hunts for his lunch, let me tell you the story I promised to share."

"You don't have to do that. I was being touchy."

"No, I do have to." She leaned forward and touched his booted foot. "I *want* to tell you."

Hayley's spirit jumped. For the first time in eight years, she truly did want to share with someone else the most painful event of her life.

The bullet crease in Sean's side burned like someone was holding a hot poker to it, but his desire to hear Hayley's story burned brighter. She sat stiff and still opposite him, seemingly studying the toes of her boots. Probably gathering her thoughts. Absently she stuck several pine nuts in her mouth, chewed, swallowed and at last looked up and met his eyes.

"I met Ryan when I was in my senior year as an art major at the College of Liberal Arts in Fairbanks. He was passionate about being an up-and-coming patrolman with the Fairbanks Police Department. A guy who was going places. He had his sights on climbing the ranks as quickly as possible. Our connection was instant, and it didn't take long before we were engaged. I was swept away by the intensity he brought to anything he did, including our relationship…or so I thought."

Her lips flatlined, and she gazed away into the trees.

"What was off about him?" Sean asked gently.

Hayley let out a dry laugh. "Pretty much everything. Turns out I misread him. For one thing, I finally figured out that I was simply a puzzle piece for him to fit into his life's master plan, but *not* a priority piece. The most important thing to him was the job."

"Law enforcement is a demanding career."

"I understand that." She nodded. "Weird— sometimes long—hours. Crime doesn't happen on a schedule. That part never bothered me, though I can't promise it wouldn't have down the road, but I never got the chance to find out how I would have coped long term."

"What happened?"

"The robbery happened."

*Robbery?* Sean adjusted his seat against the tree trunk to take pressure off the rib he suspected was broken.

"Is that pain reliever kicking in yet?" Hayley asked.

"Still in the works." He offered her a half smile. "You mentioned a robbery."

"Right. The infamous Denali Credit Union Heist a little over eight years ago."

Sean hissed in a breath, but not from pain. "I remember hearing about the incident on

the news. Nothing subtle about that job. Four
masked men stormed into the lobby with sub-
machine guns, demanding the money at the
teller stations and from the vault. A manager
at the back hit a panic button, and before the
crooks had collected all the loot, the cops had
arrived and were trying to negotiate a surrender. But the thieves were amped up on something and not dealing rationally. Things went
from bad to ugly. Innocent people were killed
before the thieves were arrested. Was your sister in the bank? Was she among the victims?"

Hayley's eyes hardened to dark marbles.
"She was a victim, but not at the bank. We
had no business being that close to the action."

"We?"

"Ryan, Kirsten and me." She drew her
knees up to her chest and hugged them.

Sean frowned. "I get why Ryan would have
been there as a cop on the scene, but what
were you and Kirsten doing—"

"The whole situation was so foolish and
unnecessary!" Hayley burst out. "Ryan wasn't
supposed to be there either. It was his day off.
Like a gallant gentleman, he'd taken Kirsten
and me out for lunch for our birthdays. On
our way home, the call about the robbery in
progress came in over the police band radio

in his car. The words electrified Ryan. He whipped the car around and headed for the bank. I asked him what he was doing, and he said he had to see if he was needed at the scene. Kirsten and I argued against going, but he insisted and we were more or less captive passengers in his car."

A fist clenched around Sean's heart. "He brought the two of you to the crime scene?"

"Not all the way. He parked two blocks back and asked us to wait for him. If he didn't return within twenty minutes that meant he was needed on-site, and we should take his car and go home. He'd catch a ride with one of his buddies. I'll never forget the manic look in his eyes. I began to realize something at that moment. The adrenaline rush of his job was more important than I was, and always would be. I was in shock with the realization. My sister was less so. She'd always seen him with a clearer lens than I did. But then, she wasn't in love with Ryan."

Hayley went silent, her stare fixed and distant.

"I can see talking about this is taking a toll on you," Sean said. "We can stop."

Her gaze snapped to his, fire in her eyes. "Stop? Not hardly! I need to finish this." Then her rigid shoulders visibly relaxed, and she let out a long breath. "Sorry. It's just been a long time since I've talked about that day. Doing it feels sort of like picking a scab off a poorly healed wound, but at the same time a healthy thing to do. Like I need to let it out to someone, and you seem like that someone."

"Okay, good." Sean nodded. "How did the situation result in your sister's death?"

Hayley offered a sad smile. "We waited in the car for about ten minutes, and then we heard gunfire. We started to debate whether we should stop waiting for Ryan and get out of there. I kept expecting to see him tearing back to us intent on whisking us away. Then the gunfire stopped, and we waited another five minutes. Shots sounded again, and Kirsten made up our minds for us by leaping out of the back seat and into the front driver's seat. She was about to put the car into gear when an armed man ran up to the car, pointed his gun at us and demanded we get out."

Sean's breath caught. "One of the robbers?"

Hayley nodded. "He'd managed to sneak out of the bank, leaving his buddies behind, and was intent on escaping capture. We happened to be sitting nearby in a running car. Ripe pickings."

A low groan escaped Sean's throat. "A car-jacking."

"Apparently, we didn't comply with his demand fast enough for this amped-up crook. As soon as Kirsten opened the door to get out of the driver's seat, the guy grabbed her, yanked her out and shoved her sprawling onto the sidewalk. I was already most of the way out of the passenger seat, one foot on the pavement and one still in the vehicle. My view of what was happening was partially blocked by the bulk of the car. But I heard the shot... I heard it." The final three words emerged in a ragged whisper.

Hayley sat, legs gripped tight to her chest, rocking like she was struggling to find her balance.

Sean's eyes grew wide, and his mouth went dry. "He shot her?"

Hayley stopped rocking and went utterly still, her eyes tightly closed. "Just like that. No warning. No reason. Then he got into the car and drove off like nothing had happened, leaving me standing in the street, staring at... my sister's...body..."

Uncaring of the pain movement cost, Sean got on his knees and went to her. As he put his arm around her, she buried her face against his chest and her shoulders began to shake. Sean's heart squeezed in on itself. Her pain and tragedy ranked every bit as profound as his. He didn't know or care how long she cried. However long she needed, that was how long she would get.

At last, she simply rested quietly against him. "I miss her so, so much every single day."

The words came out muffled against his jacket, but his heart resonated loud and clear.

"I hear you from head to toe, inside and out," Sean whispered.

Hayley lifted her head and looked at him, their faces mere inches apart. "I know you do. Perhaps that's why I could tell you."

Their breaths mingled, and he floundered to stop thinking about closing the distance and kissing her.

Then she stiffened and pulled back, her gaze wrenching away from his. "Now you also know why I don't ever consider dating a cop."

Sean's lungs went as vacant as his arms. "I'm not a cop. I'm a fed."

How pitiful did that sound, almost begging her to reconsider on a technicality?

# ELEVEN

Hayley pulled away from Sean and stood up. Her gaze swept the area. Not that she expected danger to arrive quite yet, but she needed to distract herself from the too-attractive ATF agent until she regained some semblance of composure. Without looking at him, she held down her hand to help him up, but he was already rising on his own. The soft hiss issuing between his teeth betrayed the pain movement cost him.

"We're burning daylight," she said as she hefted the pack and slung it over her shoulders. "The sun will be down in a few hours, and we'll need to stop a bit before that to set up a shelter for the night. I don't know of any cabins out this way." She headed off into the trees.

"What about Mack?" Sean's voice came from a few feet to her rear.

"He'll find us when he's ready." She resisted looking over her shoulder at him.

Did she regret baring her pain to this man? No, that wasn't the problem. It had felt natural, cathartic even, being held and allowed to cry in the arms of someone who didn't judge. Someone who wouldn't tell her—verbally or with body language—that Kirsten's death was tragic, but it had been a long time ago and she should move on.

The problem was in her wavering resolve. Part and parcel with her pain was her determination never again to risk her heart on someone whose career track kept them running toward danger. A man who might bring that danger to her doorstep.

Hadn't Sean already brought the danger—not deliberately, of course, but as a clear consequence of his job? Surely, that factor alone should strengthen her determination to remain emotionally distant from him. Yet it didn't. Quite the opposite. Sharing risk and combining effort with him to survive got her blood pumping in ways that only happened when she was swept away in creative mode with her art. The contradictory realization shot a tingle through her.

"What about your brother?"

Sean's question jerked Hayley back into the moment.

"What about Craig?"

"Since you're scheduled to speak with him every evening, and Traitor Trooper would have falsely assured him of your safety, wouldn't he have expected to hear from you last night?"

Hayley glanced over her shoulder at Sean. His dark gaze met hers. The slight V lines between his eyebrows betrayed the ongoing pain movement must be causing him.

"You're right," she said. "He would have tried to call me, expecting me to pick up this time. But since I didn't, he would have called his trooper friend again. I can't imagine what excuse Glenn could have given for my continued unavailability."

"Or maybe Glenn didn't pick up either."

"In that case, I have no doubt Craig is going frantic and reaching out to other authorities. How soon they mobilize is another question."

"But when they do, they sure won't be able to locate us out here in the bush."

"Another great reason to keep going in the direction of my homestead." Hayley redoubled her pace. "Am I moving too fast?"

"Don't you dare slow down on my account.

The painkillers have kicked in, so we need to keep our gear kicked up on high."

Hayley let out a soft chuckle. Another thing to appreciate about this guy. Whining was not in his nature, despite being wounded and thrust into an alien environment. In fact, regardless of the circumstances, he seemed to be enjoying the great outdoors.

Mack suddenly materialized like smoke wafting from the pine trees. The dog chose to trot alongside Sean rather than beside Hayley. She shot the malamute a sidelong look, and he seemed to smirk at her around his lolling tongue. Either the animal was developing a liking for the ATF agent, or he sensed Sean was wounded and was making his support available. Or maybe both. Dogs could be like that.

The snow was melting into mud that sucked at their boots, and the terrain was growing rough and all too open for Hayley's liking. Another stretch of forest loomed in the distance. They needed to reach the trees before darkness fell, but the necessity of skirting around upthrust rocks and dense clumps of thorny bushes was slowing their progress. The extra steps combined with brief steep climbs and sharp dips brought puffs of exertion from Hayley's lungs and stressed her weakened ankle. She could hardly imagine the effect on Sean with a bullet wound and a broken rib. Glancing at him, she noted white lines bracketing his mouth, but he never uttered a word of complaint.

Beside a boulder that cut the incessant wind, Hayley called a halt and passed the canteen to Sean. He drank eagerly but sparingly and returned the canteen to her. His determined smile belied the pained squint of his eyes.

"At least we don't have to worry about being spotted or attacked from the sky again," he said. "My bullets hit something that was causing them engine trouble. Best case, whoever was up there didn't make it back to your cabin."

"Not best case." Hayley frowned. "That would mean when we get there, we'll find no operational aircraft."

"Glass half-full or glass half-empty?" Sean let out a chuckle that abruptly cut off with a wince. "Let's concentrate on nabbing ourselves a sat phone and then staying out of sight until the cavalry arrives."

She shrugged. "We've been ad-libbing all along, and we're still alive."

"Let's keep it that way."

His grin teased out one of her own, and her

heart lightened. They kept going, and the terrain began to level off, though the melting snow continued to drag at their feet. At last, as dusk was creeping around them, they entered the expanse of forest. When they were well into the trees, they came to a clearing by a small meandering stream and Hayley called a halt.

Without words, Sean joined her in constructing a shelter similar to the one they'd built during the snowstorm. Only this shelter was a bit larger and featured a thick floor of pine boughs to keep them from wallowing in the mushy ground.

With their shelter built, Hayley and Sean gathered wood and Hayley used the cattail heads as tinder to help start a healthy fire. In the dense darkness, the dancing flames and crackling wood created a welcome ambience of light, heat and pleasant wood scent.

"You don't suppose our pursuers are close enough to spot this fire?" Sean asked.

Hayley wrinkled her nose and canted her head, then shook it. "I highly doubt it. Sure, the occupants of the plane that overflew us will have given them our general location, but we made good time today, despite snow and injury. Our smoke won't be visible to them at night, and besides, they will have had to stop and make their own camp by now. No more travel for them or us."

"Good enough."

Near the fire, they made themselves seats of pine boughs. At Hayley's direction, Sean gingerly settled on his seat while she collected stream water in her tall pot and set it on a hot rock just within the flames. Once the water was steaming, she popped the cattail roots into the pot to boil.

Sean frowned, eyeing the pot. "I don't know whether to be scared or intrigued about this meal we're going to eat."

Hayley sniffed. "I'll have you know I'm a five-star cattail chef."

Sean lifted both hands, palms out. "Far be it from me to disbelieve you."

"Smart man."

They both chuckled. Mack, who was stretched out on the other side of the fire, lifted his head and awarded them each a searching look, then resettled his snout on his paws and closed his eyes. Sean's stomach growled loudly, and one of the dog's eyes opened again in a definite canine glare. Hayley slapped her hands over her mouth as guffaws spouted forth.

Sean shook his head with a grin. "You'd think we were on a vacation. Next thing you know, we'll be toasting marshmallows and singing campfire songs."

"Under circumstances that didn't involve people shooting at us, this *would* actually be a fun adventure."

"I'd skip the nearly getting eaten by a bear and almost freezing to death parts, too."

"You'll get no argument from me." Hayley sobered.

Right now, right here with these companions, it was too easy to let their predicament fade from her mind. The pain of his wound must be keeping Sean all too mindful of their constant danger. She dug in the pack and came out with the painkillers.

"Take more of these," she said, handing the container to him with the canteen.

He opened the pill bottle and frowned at the contents. "We're getting low."

"There's more at the cabin."

Sean nodded but didn't lose the frown. He knew as well as she did that their very survival depended on wresting the homestead away from the intruders. They should arrive at the property by midday tomorrow. What would they find?

They were depending upon beating their armed pursuers to the homestead. Would it be possible that the hunting party on their trail could arrive there first, presenting overwhelming odds against them evicting the trespassers? That negative possibility was slim, given the fact that Glenn had a crew of tenderfeet in tow, rather than experienced wilderness trekkers. Of course, Sean wasn't experienced either, but he'd proven himself a champ.

Hayley physically shook herself. She'd grown mesmerized by her worry and her gaze into the flames. Time to eat and fortify themselves for whatever was to come. God willing, they would prevail tomorrow.

But what if God wasn't willing?

What happened to Kirsten had proven to Hayley that innocent people didn't always survive when evil actors were determined to do bad things. Tomorrow wasn't guaranteed. Would she trust God anyway? She'd been stuck on that question all these years, but she wasn't about to resolve the issue this minute.

*Time to eat.*

Using her gloves, Hayley removed the pot of boiling cattail roots from the fire and set it aside on the cool ground. With a slotted camp spoon, she scooped the roots onto a pair of tin plates.

"Butter would improve the flavor immensely," she said as she handed a steaming plate to Sean. "However, the starch will fill us up, and there are good nutrients in the roots. Let them cool a bit. You'll have to use your fingers to strip away the last of the fibrous outer coating, then go ahead and eat the center."

"Sort of like crab legs?"

She laughed. "Not at all like crab legs."

Silence fell as they worked their way through the bland meal. However, her stomach welcomed the warm bulk of the potato-textured root.

"What do you think?" she asked Sean as they finished.

"I—"

Mack's deep-throated growl cut off Sean's response as the animal lunged to his feet. Fur bristling, the dog stared over Hayley's shoulder toward the trees around their encampment. Goose bumps skittered across her skin. She turned her head and peered into the darkness. A screen of brush could not mask the eyes that gleamed back at her, firelight dancing in their feral depths.

"Wolf." The word scraped like sandpaper through her taut throat.

* * *

A shiver snaked down Sean's spine. Wolf? Slowly, he picked up the automatic rifle that had been lying by his side.

His gaze darted to Hayley. "What's the procedure here?" he asked softly, fighting to keep his tone calm and even.

"Same as with the bear." Her tone was steady but thin. "We make noise—shout, clap, whistle—but I'd rather not shoot at it. The sound of gunfire will travel far, possibly to our enemies' ears."

"Agreed." Sean nodded. "No shooting unless the animal attacks."

"Unlikely. Unless the wolf is rabid, it will run rather than attack, especially since the creature is afraid of our campfire."

"On three, we leap up and holler then."

Hayley nodded, and Sean began the countdown. On *three*, Hayley leaped to her feet and began shouting and clapping. Sean followed suit but more slowly as the pain in his side slowed his surge to his feet. The gleaming eyes winked out and underbrush rustled as the animal retreated. Tension began to ebb from Sean's shoulders. Then Mack charged forward with deep-throated barks, nearly bowling Sean over, and chased after the wolf into the trees.

"Mack! Come back here!" Hayley's shrill cry echoed through the clearing.

Face drained of color and eyes showing white all around, she sprang after her dog. Heart in his throat, Sean lunged and tackled her to the ground. Hayley squirmed to free herself as he gritted his teeth against the bright pain splintering through him and held on to her for dear life.

"Stop!" he cried in her ear, and she suddenly went still, breathing hard. "We'll have to trust Mack to handle himself. You can't run into the forest at night with a wolf out there."

"Wolves." Hayley growled the word. "Our uninvited guest probably isn't alone. They generally travel in packs."

"All the more reason to stay here by the fire and wait for Mack to return."

A little sob left her throat, and Sean's heart constricted.

"You can let me up now," she said softly. "I've got my wits about me."

Sean rolled off her, wet warmth creeping down his side. "I think I'm bleeding again." Wincing, he sat up.

"I'm so sorry." Hayley knelt at his side. "Let's move back closer to the fire. I need to stop the bleeding, disinfect that bullet crease and rebandage it."

Gingerly, Sean reclaimed his pine bough seat by the fire. He shed his jacket. His back chilled instantly, but his front remained warmed by the heat of the flames. With deft fingers, Hayley unwound the bandage from his torso, then clucked her tongue. She applied another round of the clotting aid, then packed the wound with disinfecting gauze. Sean did what he could to hold back cries of pain. She felt badly enough for causing him to reopen the wound. But, as she worked, the breath frequently hissed between his teeth.

"It's okay." Hayley spurted a wry chuckle. "If you need to yelp a little, I totally understand."

Sean barked a soft laugh but cut the sound short as the effort stabbed a sharp pang through him. "I thought we didn't need the noise because we already chased the wolf away."

Her lips formed a thin line, and she shook her head. "For now. One of us needs to be awake at all times tonight, keeping the fire stoked."

"I call dibs on the first watch. You lost sleep over me last night, so you must be exhausted."

No need to mention his own depleted condition. The pain of his wound was likely to keep him wakeful anyway.

Hayley's gaze fixed on the spot where her dog had disappeared into the forest. "I won't be able to sleep until Mack returns."

"Then let's both stand watch for a while. How about more of that tea you fixed for us this morning?"

"Good idea."

Hayley got busy with the preparations while Sean put on his jacket. Warmth stilled the shivers that had begun due to exposing his bare skin to medical ministrations. He sat still, staring into the flames, and concentrated on breathing slowly and evenly to calm the throbbing of his wound. Soon, the tea was ready, and he cradled the mug in his hands, inhaling the pleasant odor of the hot brew. Save for the crackling of the wood in the fire, silence fell over the clearing.

Then a rustle came from the bushes and Hayley jerked, slopping tea from her mug. Sean's head came up as he strained to see into the darkness. Stillness fell again, and Hayley's shoulders slumped. The words *he's okay* pressed into Sean's throat, but he couldn't let them out when he had no idea if they were true. At last, Hayley ventured a sip of her tea as her eyelids drooped.

Sean finished his mug and set it aside. He leaned forward, elbows on bent knees, and closed his eyes, drinking in the night sounds of the forest. Many nocturnal animals were out and about, creating soft sounds of movement, but nothing like the disturbance a large animal might make. No caribou or moose tonight. A slinking hunter like a wolf or a coyote might be counted upon to make little to no noise, so the proximity of a single animal or even a pack might be difficult to discern.

Abruptly, an eerie sound pierced the night. A plaintive howl stood the hairs on Sean's body straight up. The wolf was out there. Distant now. But where was Mack?

With no warning, the dog abruptly bounded into the clearing. Hayley cried out and surged to her knees even as the animal ran straight toward her and bowled her over onto her back. Feminine laughter and spluttering filled the air as the malamute swiped his big, pink tongue all over her face. Sean defied the pain in his ribs to add his chuckles to the mix. When, finally, Hayley managed to sit up, Mack left her and trotted over to Sean.

He lifted a hand and gripped the animal's

ruff. "No knocking me over or licking my face," he said, ruffling the fur on Mack's head, "but I'm very glad to see you."

The malamute defied the prohibition and managed a swipe to Sean's nose. Then he turned away and settled down beside Hayley, head held high with a distinct air of accomplishment.

Sean mock-glowered at him. "I suppose you think you chased the wolf away."

Mack answered with a decisive *woof.*

"Well, okay then."

Sean grinned at Hayley, and she grinned back as she buried a hand in her dog's thick fur.

"Why don't you go ahead and get some rest." Sean tilted his head toward their shelter.

"Don't mind if I do." Hayley nodded. "Wake me for my turn at watch after midnight when the moon touches the treetops."

"You got it."

Hayley awarded him a soft smile that turned Sean's heart to mush. Then she retired with Mack to their bed of pine boughs.

As quiet again descended over the clearing, Sean's shoulders slumped. They had survived thus far against overwhelming opposition both in manpower and firepower, but he couldn't kid himself that he and Hayley weren't now running on fumes, physically and mentally. Yet tomorrow they would face the most critical battle yet—retaking her cabin and acquiring a means of communicating with the outside world.

Despite Craig's concern for his sister, there was no guarantee anyone was heading to the rescue. It was best to figure they were on their own and plan accordingly. But what was the plan? Yes, they knew the objectives, but how to accomplish them wouldn't become apparent until they reached the cabin and discerned the situation. He'd been assuming only Patterson and the airplane pilot were holding down the fort there, but those numbers weren't guaranteed. It was also possible his shots at the plane had injured someone aboard, not just the aircraft itself. Again, until they arrived on-site, they wouldn't know for sure.

As an undercover agent, improvising in the moment was a necessary second-nature talent, but now he had more than himself to think and plan for. How would he be able to live with himself if he failed to protect Hayley and deliver her out of this situation with a whole skin? Not well. Not well at all.

How would he be able to live, period, if

they *did* survive and come through to safety and they said goodbye to each other? The breath bottled up in Sean's chest.

She would go her own way. She'd made that abundantly clear. He'd be alone again. His usual condition ever since his mom died and his dad checked out emotionally. He'd grown accustomed to the alone status, figuring it an unchangeable factor of his life. But now that Hayley had stirred his heart like no other woman, the loneliness would be an acute misery, like living with chronic pain.

Sean reached out and took a chunk of wood from the pile near the fire. He stirred the embers, then added the fresh chunk and several others. Soon, the campfire roared and crackled merrily, mocking the heaviness in his heart.

*Get your head right*, Sean told himself.

Tomorrow could well be a day of great danger. He needed to stay sharp and focused. They had to win. If only he didn't dread the aftermath of victory more than the coming battle itself.

# TWELVE

Hayley's pleasant sepia-toned dream of walking through a summer meadow, hand in hand with some unknown person she never turned her head to see, melted away under a firm grip on her shoulder that gently shook her awake. Her eyes popped open, and she gasped at the bearded face hovering near hers. *Who? What?* Then reality clicked into place. Sean. Tension unwound from her muscles.

"Sorry to startle you." His teeth flashed in a brief grin. "The moon is halfway down into the trees. You were sleeping so well. I hated to wake you."

"Apology unnecessary." Hayley sat up beside him, the top of her head lightly brushing the boughs of their shelter. "I was wandering in dreamland."

No way was she going to explain that statement more thoroughly. Not when she harbored a niggling suspicion that the hand in hers had been his—and that their togetherness had felt utterly right.

"I made more tea," he said.

"Perfect. You get some rest now." She patted his sturdy shoulder and scooted out of the shelter.

Mack was sitting by the fire, regarding her solemnly.

"Good not-quite-morning to you, sir," she said to him.

The dog swished his tail across the ground in an abbreviated wag. She took a cross-legged seat beside him and patted his big head. Appreciation rumbled from his chest. Then she poured herself a mug of the tea steaming by the fire. Her gaze scanned the area and her ears sought feedback. Soon, she relaxed, hearing and seeing nothing out of the ordinary.

Soft huffing and small movements from their shelter indicated Sean settling himself onto the pine bough bed, resting on his un-injured side. Then he went still, and all that showed of him were the bottoms of his boots.

The air had warmed significantly from yesterday's snowy bluster, but still the breeze was cool enough to chill her cheeks. The tea mug sent warmth through her hands and up her arms while the tea itself warmed her insides. However, her stomach let out a low growl for sustenance liquid alone could not satisfy.

Hayley took the hunting knife from the pack and stepped to the edge of the clearing where several sturdy white spruce trees stood sentinel. With the knife's edge, she scored vertical lines through the rough outer bark then sliced horizontally at the bottom and top of each set of vertical lines. With the cuts in place, peeling away the outer bark was simple, exposing edible white inner bark that she quickly harvested. Repeating the process on several trunks, she soon possessed a nutritious meal for Sean and herself without inflicting lasting damage on the trees. The white inner bark she'd taken possessed anti-inflammatory properties that would help them both in their healing processes.

She boiled some of the bark for herself and ate it but left the rest to prepare for Sean when she roused him at dawn. He would receive only a few hours of sleep this night, but the coming day promised enough action to keep anyone awake. Hayley shivered though she wasn't cold. Would the next night find them resting in comfort, safety and warmth? Or would they wind up cold and lifeless as the bare ground?

Hayley firmed her jaw. She couldn't think like that. Nor could she allow herself to ponder the invitation to the ongoing relationship Sean seemed to be issuing. No matter that she found him attractive on every level. Her heart couldn't handle the potential cost of opening her life to him.

Then again, in refusing to risk herself, wasn't she choosing to remain alone and lonely? Hadn't she been making that choice for years now? What would Kirsten think? A deep ache spread through her core. The loss of her twin sister as a human sounding board had left an unfathomable void in her life.

Would Sean be able to fill that void? She shrugged off the question. It would be grossly unfair to him and to herself to cast any person in the role of completer. In a sense, she'd made this mistake in her relationship with Kirsten, but that had effectively been a consequence of family biology dating from birth rather than a conscious choice.

Yet talking to Sean about Kirsten and allowing him to hold her as she cried had changed something inside her. Opened her eyes. Her conscious choice since the loss of her twin sister had been to close off her relationship options with other people and to constrict her relationship with God. Healthy those choices were not.

Hayley looked upward into the star-strewn sky. The moon was long down past the horizon, but even as she gazed, luminescent streaks and swirls of greenish light began to flicker across the sky. The aurora borealis had awakened. The majestic light show intensified and throbbed through her as if it had become one with her pulse—or her pulse one with it. The beauty would never grow old for her, nor would she want to be away from it for long. But tonight, as the colors morphed in shade and vividness through a gamut of greens, pinks, blues and purples, the majesty humbled her.

Did she even possess the strength to change? Sean seemed to think she was strong, but he was mistaken. She was a mess, a turmoil of weakness and fear. If she didn't get control of her emotions, she could get them both killed.

*God, please help me.*

The prayer was weak—thin as broth—but the best she could muster. The most consciously sincere prayer she'd mustered since Kirsten died. A step in the right direction? Time would tell. At least, the fist-like pressure around her heart loosened, and she was able to take in a full breath of crisp air tinged with woodsmoke, pine needles and moist earth.

"Wow!"

Sean's muted exclamation drew her attention toward their shelter. He stood outside the entrance, hands on hips, staring up at the majestic dance of lights.

Hayley stood up. "You get the aurora in Oregon, too, don't you?"

"On occasion," Sean answered, without taking his attention from the sky. "But not like this."

"I thought you were sleeping," she said.

"Easier said than done." His gaze met hers. "My body is exhausted, but my mind won't shut down."

"How does your wound feel?"

Sean grimaced. "Uncomfortable, but not intolerable. I'll lie down again, but I'm glad I got to see that." He motioned toward the sky.

"Me, too." Despite the hardships felt throughout her body and mind, a genuine smile broke forth on her lips.

"Stunning," Sean mumbled as his gaze fell away from hers, and he returned to their shelter.

Hayley's heart bumped against her ribs. Of course, he was referring to the aurora borealis. Wasn't he?

She sat hunched at the fire, sipping tea and keeping the flames stoked. Near at hand, the soft burble of the stream lulled her senses. Rustles from the forest betrayed the movements of nocturnal creatures great and small. A distant eerie scream roused her from a semi-stupor and raised the hairs at the nape of her neck. Lynx. The predatory cat was unlikely to prowl too closely to humans or their campfire. The wolf was more of a danger to them, especially if he was not a lobo but with a pack. However, there had been no more lupine howls, either near or far away. Hopefully, the creature had been spooked by their earlier run-in and was now long gone, along with any others that might be with him.

A sharp blast followed by a series of staccato bursts brought Hayley surging to her feet. The breath stalled in her lungs. Gunfire. Faint and distant, yet all too close. Their enemies had anticipated the dawn and were closing in on them.

\* \* \*

Sean jerked awake, every muscle tense. The pain from his wound ground through him, but he had no time to care. Supporting the broken rib by holding his left arm tight against his side, he wormed his way out of the shelter and onto his feet.

"Gunfire," he said. "Our pursuers. Spooked by wildlife. Possibly our wolf or his pack?"

Hayley nodded, already in action, dousing the fire with water from the nearby stream. However, she'd set aside a pair of narrow logs, flaming at the ends. He didn't stop to ask her reasons for preserving torches. She'd tell him soon enough. Sean collected belongings and made sure they were stowed in the pack. Mack pranced around them ready to go, clearly sensing the urgency.

"We've got to stay as far ahead of them as possible," Hayley said, taking the heavy pack from him as he was clearly not fit to carry it. She handed him his automatic weapon and a torch. "Through the remainder of the night, fire will help hold predators at bay as we move."

Sean nodded. "If we keep sufficient distance between Traitor Trooper's bunch and us, they won't be able to see the fire, and we can ditch the torches—"

"At sunup." Hayley's smile flickered. "No moss growing on your wits, Special Agent."

He snorted and instantly regretted the ambitious use of his lungs. His broken rib was a major liability, but he couldn't let it slow them down. They were mere hours away from Hayley's homestead and an impending gunfight. Dangerous by anyone's estimation, but not nearly as dangerous as allowing the larger party to catch up to them.

Hayley led the way into the forest. Sean followed on her heels, eyes sharp for obstacles that could trip them up or predators that could attack. Mack ranged in a circular zigzag around them—sometimes ahead, sometimes behind, as if guarding the perimeter. The aurora borealis had subsided, leaving the atmosphere truly dark. Even starlight filtered faintly through the tree branches. The light of the torches was welcome and necessary for safe travel. They could have used the camp lantern for illumination, but it was fire that kept wild animals at bay.

Progress was steady but not swift. Sean mentally gave thanks that the terrain was rolling, with periods of gently sloping downward and then sloping upward, rather than steep or rough. Miles flowed uneventfully beneath their feet until, at last, a pinkening sky lessened their dependence on torchlight. Another stream bisected their path, and Hayley asked for his nubbin of flaming log. She doused them both in the water and tossed the wood aside.

"How close are we to your homestead?" Sean asked.

"Close. Only a few miles. We should stop and hydrate and eat something." She led the way to a fallen log and sat down with a heavy sigh.

Sean perched gingerly beside her but denied his face the right to wince. Kowtowing to pain wasn't on the agenda for the next few hours when they went to battle.

"They're going to know we're coming," he told Hayley. "We need to have—"

"A plan. Yes, I know." She dug a clear, plastic bag out of the pack. The bag contained strips of some sort of white substance. "Here. Eat this. I harvested and cooked it last night. It's cold now and won't taste great, but it's good nutrition that will give you energy."

Sean took the bag from her and regarded the pale offering inside of it with a furrowed brow. "What is it?"

"Boiled pine bark."

He shot her a sharp glance. "You've got to be kidding me."

"Wilderness survival is serious business," Hayley laughed, belying her words. "I ate my share while you were sleeping."

Sean opened the bag, reached in and pinched off a portion of a strip of bark. He brought the piece to his nose, sniffed it, then quickly popped it into his mouth, chewed and swallowed.

Hayley's gaze never left his face. "What do you think?"

"Tastes like slightly moist, vaguely sweet sawdust."

Her laughter rang out again. "Apt description. That's pretty much what you've eaten. Though I defy you to tell me when you've ever actually ingested sawdust."

"I did just now." He eyed her blandly.

"Smart aleck." Hayley dug out the bag of pine nuts and joined him in consuming breakfast.

They sat in comfortable silence, eating, as the morning birds chorused around them. Mack silently disappeared into the trees. Sean finished what he could stomach of the soggy tree bark, then handed the bag back to Hayley.

Their fingers brushed as she took the bag

from him, and something like a mild shock went through him, like what sometimes happened when a person scuffed their feet across a rug and then touched something. Her taut expression gave no indication that she had felt the electrical connection, too.

Sean studied her face. She was pale, except where the cool breeze had whipped color into her cheeks. Her eyes were dark—pensive. Worry lines drew her eyebrows toward each other, and the tip of her tongue was caught between her teeth.

"We're going to make it," he told her softly.

Her gaze lasered into his. "You can't guarantee that."

"No, but a confrontation entered into without hope and determination is a confrontation automatically lost."

Her forehead smoothed, and the edges of her lips tilted slightly upward. "Sounds like the sort of proverb my brother would spout in a sticky situation."

"I don't know about that, but I do know I have faith in your courage and steadiness under fire."

She let out a sharp scoffing sound. "I'm glad of your faith because I haven't had faith in anything for a very long time."

"Then change the decision."

"You want me to decide to believe? Just like that?"

"Yup."

Her shoulders rolled, and she straightened her spine. "Okay." Her tone carried notes of wonder and trepidation, but also resolve.

"So, what's the plan?" He gazed down at her. "They know we're coming. Any surprise attack was blown out of the water when they overflew us yesterday."

A hint of mischief entered Hayley's gaze. "They may know we're coming, but they'll never see us until it's too late."

Sean cocked a brow. "Do tell."

"Come on." She surged up from the fallen tree trunk. "I'll explain en route. Let's hurry."

Adjusting the strap of his rifle across his chest, Sean followed her rapid steps. A slight grin stretched his lips. When this woman made up her mind to do something, obstacles would be stupid not to get out of her way. What sort of devious trick did she have in mind now? One thing was sure: being around Hayley was never dull, though a bit mysterious at times.

"What's this 'never see us' option you've got going?" Sean asked when they were well underway.

"We come in through the cellar," she answered without slowing pace or glancing over her shoulder.

"Your cabin has a cellar?"

"Indeed, it does. An old root cellar—dirt floor, dank cement walls. It's original with the first cabin built on the property. The current cabin is a significant expansion of the original, and modern amenities negated the usefulness of the cellar, so we never go down there. But it still exists, accessible under a trapdoor in the kitchen."

"And the cellar's existence helps us how?"

"There's an old outside entrance. Sort of like the storm cellar setup you sometimes see in the Midwest Lower 48."

They came to a sparsely wooded area, and Sean hustled up to stride beside Hayley. Mack must have sneaked up behind them because he suddenly trotted past, proceeding ahead of them with his tongue lolling and tail wagging.

"Somebody's a happy camper," Sean said.

"Successful hunt I expect," Hayley answered.

"Back on topic. I get it about the root cellar, but I don't get how we reach the outer door and sneak into it without being seen. By now, Patterson and company will have locked and/or barricaded every entrance and will be keeping a close watch on approaches to the place. And they'll know we can't wait for the cover of darkness to attack. The hunters behind us will catch up before then, and we'll be caught in a pincher."

Hayley stopped walking. Sean brought himself to an abrupt halt facing her.

She glared up at him, hands on hips. "Pull your weight, Mr. Hope and Determination. I thought of the cellar, now you think of a way for us to get to it."

Sean opened his mouth, then shut it again. No words came. Then his thoughts surged past the speed bumps of difficulties his imagination had conjured.

"We'll need a distraction," he said.

"Something to keep their focus elsewhere while we—"

"Access the house."

"Right." Hayley nodded decisively. "When you figure out what that is, let me know." She turned and set off even faster than before. "You've got about an hour to prove yourself a tactical genius."

Tactical genius? Sean shook his head as he limp-trotted after her, hugging his broken rib. He needed to come up with a distraction, but *she* was a distraction when he had to think objectively. His toe hit a hidden rock in the ground, and he stumbled, hissing against a stab of pain in his side. Righting himself, he barely caught sight of her slender figure disappearing ahead of him through a seemingly infinitesimal gap between trees.

A thin smile took form on his lips. Then again, perhaps she was exactly the distraction necessary.

# THIRTEEN

*Keep moving*, Hayley ordered feet that wanted to slow down—to put off the coming confrontation. She'd spoken glibly to Sean about coming up with a plan of attack, but that tone was to mask the dread roiling in her belly.

They were headed into a gunfight, plain and simple. Sure, she'd experienced one of those two days ago, but she'd been firing at her cabin, an inanimate object, without actually *seeing* the enemy other than the answering gun flashes. This time, she might have to point and shoot at people she was looking at eye-to-eye.

Could she pull the trigger? How could she not if it meant survival for Sean and herself? Sean was depending on her to be up to the task.

Soft footfalls heralded the agent moving up

to stride at her heels. The guy's woodcraft had definitely improved over the days they'd been on the run. She'd barely heard his approach.

Hayley glanced over her shoulder at him. His scowl reflected deep thought. Had he come up with a plan already?

"What?" she said.

"This outside access to the root cellar— what side of the house is it on? How visible is it to someone on high alert, watching for the approach of hostiles?"

"The door is located against the narrower side of the house next to the kitchen."

"So, anyone watching the rear kitchen entrance wouldn't be able to see it."

"Not from the doorway, but a watcher could easily catch sight of someone approaching through the kitchen window over the sink."

Sean let out a soft grunt and went back to abstracted scowling.

"Something's percolating in that head of yours," Hayley said.

"Is the cellar door locked?"

"Not locked per se. A two-by-four of wood is stuck through the twin handles of the side-by-side doors. Out here, we're not as focused on keeping human intruders out as we are bent on blocking the invasion of four-footed critters."

Sean nodded. "Good. Then I won't have to deal with a chain or padlock."

"*You* won't have to deal with them? I thought we were in this together."

"You assigned me to come up with an entry plan, and that's what I'm doing. Your part is to reprise your role as a distraction while I slip into the house and deal with Patterson and the pilot."

Hayley frowned. She hadn't anticipated them splitting up for the attack, but maybe Sean's idea was the best way—perhaps the only way that stood a chance of working. Or maybe she was telling herself that because the splitting up approach lessened the likelihood she might have to shoot someone. All to the good.

Unless Sean got killed in the execution of the plan. The greater risk was certainly his. Was she okay with that?

Her heart panged. No, she wasn't okay with that at all. Not simply in the generic sense that she would mourn the loss of human life. No, this loss would be personal. Again, not simply in the sense that she knew and esteemed Sean as a capable officer of the law. No, losing him would rip her heart out. She could no longer pretend otherwise. Did that mean she cared for this man on a level that defied her rule never again to become involved with someone in a law enforcement career?

"Once I'm in the cellar," Sean said, "other than guys with guns, what kind of problems am I going to have with getting into the cabin proper through the kitchen floor?"

His question jerked Hayley from her internal debate.

"What? Oh." She mentally shook herself. This was no time to contemplate an ill-advised romantic interest. "There's no lock on the trapdoor, inside or outside. We designed the hatch to blend almost seamlessly with the rest of the hardwood floor. It opens up under the kitchen table."

"No rug on top of the door?"

"Nope."

"Excellent." A wolfish grin showed white teeth rimmed by his dark beard and mustache. "The table may camouflage the movement of the door. Still, speed will be of the essence once I emerge into the cabin."

"What exactly do I do to provide a distraction? Start shooting at the cabin like last time?"

Sean shook his head. "Patterson is sharp. If we do the same thing as we did before when I raced for the airplanes, his mind will immediately scream at him that we're trying to divert him from the real action. No, we've got to make him think you, Mack and I are together and trying to assault them in the cabin. If he catches on that I'm not with you, he'll be looking out for me to come at them from another direction and that will negate any advantage we might have."

"But how will we spoof him into believing you're with me?"

"Scarecrow."

"Huh?" Hayley stopped and faced Sean with her hands on her hips. "Do you mind being a tad less cryptic?"

"Operation Scarecrow. In my mind—" he tapped the side of his head "—that's how I'm thinking of this ploy. We're going to make a stick figure that mimics me in height and put my coat on it with the hood pulled up."

Hayley snorted. "How long do you think a wooden scarecrow is going to fool anybody?"

"From a distance? Long enough. Hopefully. Perhaps longer than you might think if we do this right."

"And what is this *right* way?"

"When you figure out what that is, let me know." Sean chuckled and moved off into the woods.

"Turnabout is *not* fair play," she called.

Then again, maybe it was. As she started after him, her thoughts began toying with ideas. They'd scarcely been walking another half mile when the edge of the forest loomed. The back of her workshop came into sight with the homestead cabin standing at a right angle to the left of it and about twenty yards distant. Through the screen of trees, the corner of the cabin was barely visible, though the odor of woodsmoke and a plume of gray marking the blue sky above signified the cabin's occupants were keeping the fireplace stoked.

Hayley halted with Sean by her side. Mack came up to them also and sat down at her feet.

"Here we are." Sean's tone came out rough like his throat was constricted.

Hayley could hardly blame him. Her own throat had gone so tight she wasn't sure she could utter a word. Showdown coming right up. Would the next minutes see them still alive?

A warm hand gripped her shoulder, and she turned to find Sean gazing sternly down upon her. "We can do this."

"We *have* to do this," she whispered.

He nodded, and she nodded back.

"The root cellar entrance is on the side of the cabin only a few yards distant from the woods," Hayley said. "You should be able to retain cover until you're standing in line with the double doors. But then you'll have to make a run for it in the open to get there."

"I'm going to need noise cover while I access the cellar. I'm guessing the hinges on those doors might creak."

"Good guess. I don't think Craig or I have oiled those hinges in recent history. Let's get busy making the very special ATF agent scarecrow."

Sean let out a snort as he picked up a long stick from the ground. "You'll have to walk Mr. Faux Agent along the edge of the forest, allowing glimpses of him and you until you get some kind of a response from the cabin—either a yell or possibly even gunfire. Then feel free to return fire, keeping up the noise factor." He halted his stick-gathering enterprise and met Hayley's gaze. "Make sure the scarecrow is the more exposed of the two of you."

"Don't worry. I've got that part fixed in my mind. And Mack—" she looked down at her dog "—you stay right there."

She pointed to the patch of ground where he was sitting. A shudder rippled through her, imagining her dog running out of the tree line into gunfire. Mack let out a rumble in his chest and hunkered down, fully prone.

Without another word, Hayley and Sean went about collecting sturdy sticks and lashing together a wooden cross that came to roughly Sean's height. He shrugged out of his jacket with only a minor wince.

"We haven't had a chance to check your injury today," she said. "Are you going to be able to lift those doors and move as quickly as you need to do?"

"I don't have the luxury of coddling myself. I'll do what needs to be done."

Of that, Hayley had no doubt. She swallowed any further protests.

Sean draped his jacket around the crossbeam and flipped the hood over the top of the upright beam. The effect was remarkable. A distant onlooker could easily believe they were seeing a human being, especially when the figure was also partially cloaked by forest vegetation.

"This is actually a genius idea." She flickered a smile at Sean.

"Why, thank you, ma'am." He executed a

mock-courtly bow, accompanied by another barely discernible wince.

"Don't let the compliment go to your head." She glared at him. "We still have to survive this mess."

He stood close, gazing down at her. His dark eyes went darker still. Intense and consuming, yet warm and welcoming. Something like steel bars around Hayley's heart softened—melting away like a mirage.

"That's why I have to do this right now." Sean's words emerged in a hoarse whisper.

His strong arms gathered her close, and his mouth captured hers. Nothing in Hayley mounted a resistance. Only a faint, cold voice—spewing fear and caution—echoed tinnily in her brain. But this time, the familiar litany sounded like an enemy, not the friend keeping her safe that she'd mistaken it for these many years. Her arms went around Sean's neck, and she returned the kiss.

Then suddenly, her arms were empty. The breeze chilled her lips as his tall, sturdy figure disappeared into the trees, heading toward mortal danger. Her heart rent in two.

*Please, God, keep him safe. Bring him back to me. Maybe I'm ready to risk my heart again after all.*

\* \* \*

The heart-melting sensation of Hayley in his arms, their lips pressed together, lingered with Sean as he glided through the forest in the direction of the cabin. He mentally shook off the beguiling distraction even as the cold gripped him in chilly fingers. The lack of a jacket made a huge difference in coping with the fall weather in the Alaskan bush.

Sean drew parallel with the cabin and stopped walking. Through the screen of trees and bushes, he made out the log siding and, framed by it, the kitchen window. No human figure appeared beyond the glass, though that circumstance could change at any moment. However, a pair of boards had been affixed across the opening on the inside, effectively preventing that means of access to the cabin but also restricting the enemies' view. Good thing crawling through the kitchen window had never been the plan.

Beneath the window, the large cellar doors of weathered wood angled against the cabin only a foot or two above the ground. As Hayley had said, the doors were held shut by a small length of two-by-four thrust between the handles.

Tension rippled through Sean's muscles.

Once he broke tree cover, he would be in plain sight for half a dozen yards before he reached the cellar doors and then until he opened them and ducked down into the cellar. Sean pulled his cell phone from his pocket and powered it up. Significant battery life remained because they'd kept their useless phones off for most of the past three days. The flashlight app would be vital once he entered the dark cellar. He'd preferred the small device to toting along the camping lamp from Hayley's pack.

Sean returned the phone to his pocket and checked the load on his automatic, then did the same with the handgun he'd stuck in the waistband of his jeans against the small of his back. His preparations appeared to be in order. Now, he could only wait for their diversion to be noticed by the occupants of the cabin.

A deep-throated bark, followed by a woman's outcry, drew his attention in Hayley's direction. The commotion brought a swift reaction from the cabin. An automatic rifle chattered from the front of the structure, answered by gunfire from the woods. Hayley had done her part, now Sean needed to do his.

Inhaling a deep breath of brisk, pine-laden

air, he charged from the protection of the trees and covered the distance to the cellar entrance with long strides that sent shards of pain through his wounded side. But the pain faded quickly as adrenaline rushed through his system. He reached the doors and ripped the two-by-four from its position, then threw it to the side.

His two-handed grip closed around one of the metal handles, and his whole body went rigid as he heaved against the heavy door. The rusty hinges creaked, but not as badly as he had anticipated. The door sprang open, and a blast of musty air bathed his face from the darkness below.

Even adrenaline couldn't entirely mask the sharp protest the effort drew from his broken rib. Warmth sprang forth from the area. He'd probably torn the wound open and was bleeding again. None of that mattered.

Sean retrieved his phone and pointed the flashlight down into the dark pit, revealing a set of rickety-looking wooden stairs leading to a bare dirt floor. With no time to second-guess the plan, he entrusted himself to the steps, proceeding with controlled haste. The wood creaked beneath his feet but did not collapse.

Frowning, he glanced back over his shoulder toward the ground-level opening. He had no time or ability to close the doors. Hopefully, their enemies would remain ignorant of the entrance and not notice the open portal.

Reaching the cellar floor, Sean panned the flashlight around the small room. At his height, the narrow-beamed ceiling hovered mere inches above the top of his head. The dank-smelling space probably encompassed less square footage than the modern kitchen above. Dusty, empty canning jars sat on wooden shelving against cement walls, but otherwise, the area was bare. Ahead of him, a ladderlike set of stairs led upward to a square hatch that might prove a tight squeeze for his shoulders.

Sean stilled his breathing and listened. Sporadic gunfire continued aboveground, but no one seemed to be walking across the kitchen floor. Hopefully, the bad guys' attention was entirely on the woods behind the workshop.

*Good job, Hayley.*

Swiftly, Sean strode to the steep stairs. He'd only need to step up once to start pressing against the hatch, but the narrow step would need to fully hold his weight. A crack in the center of the wood slab put that prospect into question. Sean skipped that stair and entrusted himself to the second one, which required him to hunch beneath the trapdoor.

Holding his breath, he pressed head, hands and shoulders against the hatch. With a soft grumble, it moved and he brought his eyes level with the hardwood flooring in the kitchen area. Above, the table threw a shadow into his field of view, but no human legs and shoes nearby betrayed the presence of Patterson or whoever else was with the arms-trafficking kingpin.

So far, so good.

Sean pressed harder against the hatch with his shoulders even as he drew the handgun from behind his back. In close quarters, this type of firepower should be more than sufficient. The moment he had room enough, he wriggled his entire body out and onto the kitchen floor but left one booted foot in the hatchway to keep the trapdoor from banging into place.

Still, no attention was paid to him. Sean swiftly sat up and manually lowered the hatch door. Then he crawled from beneath the table and rose silently to his feet. His adversaries were out of sight, likely in the living room. He glanced around the kitchen, noting the reason Patterson didn't seem concerned about anyone bursting in through the rear door. It had been barricaded by a pair of wooden planks nailed into the doorframe.

A few growled curse words floated to him from the front of the cabin, followed by a loud blast of automatic gunfire. A bitter, metallic tang hung in the air from all the shooting.

"Stop wasting ammo!" Patterson's voice snarled. "They know they're not getting in here, and Glenn's crew will be along soon enough to put an end to them."

"Yeah? And then how are we going to escape from the back of nowhere?" another voice whined, one Sean recognized. Rudy Spiegel, the gang's pilot. "Our last operable plane is shot up."

"Relax. It still flies."

"Barely."

"We only have to limp into Nenana. Glenn will get us fresh wings there."

Sean let out a slow breath. The trooper's plane remained airworthy. At least to an extent. Good to know.

He chanced a step toward the living room. Thankfully, the floor didn't creak. A big pat on the back to Craig and Hayley, who had made their updates to the cabin solid and sturdy.

Another cautious step brought Sean in view of the enemy. They stood a few feet from one another, facing away from him. Both peered outside through holes made in the plywood sheet that had been used to cover the opening of the shattered picture window.

"Go check all windows and doors," Patterson ordered his minion.

"Ah, boss, everything except the front door is boarded up tighter than a drum."

"Just do it!"

His adversaries were armed, but they were standing with their backs to him, giving him the advantage. They'd never have time to whirl and shoot at him. Sean took another step forward, giving himself the best angle possible to cover them.

"Better yet," he barked at the pair, "don't move a muscle."

Both men jerked stiffly. Rudy let out a snarl and made as if to turn. Sean pressed the trigger and sent a bullet into the plywood next to his head. The man yelped and clapped a hand to his cheek where splinters must have scored his skin.

"Drop the guns to the floor," Sean directed,

"and then face me slowly with your hands locked behind your heads."

A staccato clatter signaled obedience to his first command. Grumbling curse words, Rudy put his hands behind his head and slowly began to turn, but Patterson stood with his hands raised, looking back at Sean across his shoulder.

"ATF, I presume," the lead weapon's trafficker said in the exaggeratedly suave tone that Sean had learned to identify as a symptom of this man's extreme aggravation. "They've tried to infiltrate my organization before, but you are the only agent who succeeded. I'm impressed."

"Yes, I'm ATF, but I don't want your worthless compliments, just compliance. Unless you'd prefer me to spray wood splinters into your face, too…or better yet, put one through a limb you might be fond of."

With a long huff, Patterson locked his fingers behind his head and turned fully to face Sean. The pair of crooks glared at him as he moved farther into the room and came around the bullet-shredded sofa. Sean spotted the men's guns on the floor and kicked them well away.

"Now," he said, "on your knees—slowly— and then cross your ankles over each other."

The men complied, and Sean backed away toward the front door. Time to invite Hayley and Mack to join the party.

"If you don't mind," Patterson said through the teeth-gritted snarl on his face, "I'd like to know how you got in here."

"I do mind. I don't owe you any explanation. But I will tell you this—you're under arrest." He began to recite the Miranda warning as he opened the door. He darted a glance outside and then returned his attention to his prisoners. "Come on in, Hayley," he shouted out.

Moments later, her slim figure left the tree line at a run with Mack on her heels. "I hear people approaching through the trees," she called as she neared the porch.

Abruptly, a tsunami of gunfire erupted from the forest. Hayley stutter-stepped and fell face-first onto the porch. Sean's gut plunged into his toes. Had they come this close to safety only to be gunned down now?

# FOURTEEN

Hayley turned her head and absorbed most of her forward fall on her jacket-padded arms, yet her cheek still struck the porch boards a glancing blow. Pain slapped her face, but nowhere else on her body registered discomfort. Had she been struck by a bullet? Apparently not. In her rush to flee her murderous pursuers and gain the shelter of the cabin, she'd misjudged the height of the steps and caught her toe on the edge of the stairs. Perhaps the fall had actually saved her from being shot.

She started to scramble to her knees, but something grabbed the hood of her jacket and dragged her over the threshold into the cabin. The furry paws near her face revealed her rescuer to be Mack. Someone, probably Sean, slammed the door closed on the continuing cacophony of gunfire from the woods.

Male shouts from within the cabin and

the smack of something hard striking flesh brought her head up, and she rolled into a sitting position. Sean stood over one scowling man who was on his knees and another clutching his head but flat on his back.

"Are you all right?" Sean glanced over his shoulder at her.

"Fine." She didn't bother to mention the bump on her cheek, though the flesh over her cheekbone was warm and starting to swell. "I'm not shot or anything serious, just clumsy climbing the stairs. Are *you* all right?"

"Doing good. But one of these yo-yos tried to scramble for his weapon when I took my eyes off him for a second to make sure you got inside. I had to hit him with the butt of the rifle."

Hayley's gaze fell on the man curled in a ball and cradling his head. The goon should be thankful Sean had merely struck him and not shot him. The fierce scowl on the other man's face, the one on his knees, reflected no form of gratitude. This guy in the rumpled suit must be Patterson, the ruthless leader of the weapons smugglers. Hayley met his cold blue gaze and shivered. The man would like nothing better than to put Sean and her down like rabid dogs.

*Not going to happen.* Hayley struggled to her feet and returned Patterson's glare.

"Look for the sat phone," Sean said tersely.

"On it."

Her gaze swept the bullet-riddled room. Major repairs to walls and replacement of windows and furnishings would be necessary. Her fists clenched. How dare these crooks barge into her home and wreak havoc? Not to mention threatening life and limb?

There! The satellite phone was on the desk. Hayley strode over and snatched it up. Finally, they could call for help. Then she paused. Should she call her brother first and have him contact Nenana or Fairbanks authorities? Or should she contact the authorities herself? With her brother's friend Glenn turning out to be in Patterson's pay, how could she be sure she could trust people at the Troopers' headquarters?

"Call your brother and alert him and then get ahold of Fairbanks," Sean said. "Patterson's reach into law enforcement there can't be too deep. This isn't his usual stomping ground."

Hayley jerked a nod in his direction and punched in her brother's number. The call rang and then rang again.

"Who is this?" a familiar voice snapped through the headset.

Hayley's heart soared. "Craig, it's me."

"Thank the Lord." The relief in her brother's tone weighed a ton. "I've been so worried."

"You still should be. A federal agent and I are under attack by a gang of smugglers at our cabin."

"Attack!" The word exploded through the speaker. "Two nights ago, Glenn assured me you were fine, but then you didn't pick up my call again last night. I tried to reach Glenn once more, but he didn't pick up either."

A lump grew in Hayley's throat. Her brother was going to be devastated about his friend. "That's just it." Her tone came out hoarse. "Glenn's working with the crooks."

Silence answered her pronouncement, then a strangled gurgle. "Are you sure?"

"He's been the lead tracker for the gang while the agent and I were on the run from them in the bush for the past two days. Only minutes ago, we retook the cabin, but the battle isn't over. There's a crew of them outside trying to overrun us. We need help!"

"I'm on my way."

"No, we need help immediately. Not whenever you can get here from Seattle."

"And I mean I'm literally on my way right now. I left Seattle last night, and I'm in the air on the last leg of the journey to the cabin. I'm about twenty minutes out with a trooper from Fairbanks."

A fist squeezed Hayley's heart. "Are you sure you can trust the guy?"

"I imagine we'll soon discover the answer. How long can you hold out?"

"I don't know, but we're going to—"

A noise from the kitchen halted Hayley's words. She turned to discover the source of the sound. A man's head was popping up through the kitchen floor hatch. Their enemies had discovered the cellar entrance. She should have thought to blockade the trapdoor before she made her call.

Heart hammering against her ribs, Hayley dropped the phone and brought her gun up. Her finger froze on the trigger as Mack scrambled past her, snarling and snapping at the intruder. The dog's bulky body blocked her line of fire. However, the gang member wasn't about to brave a ferocious dog attack, and the hatch thumped shut as the man retreated.

Hayley commanded Mack to come to her, and the dog obeyed, even as whatever enemies were in the cellar opened fire, peppering holes in the kitchen floor. Had Mack not obediently left the room, he would almost certainly have been shot. Gritting her teeth, Hayley returned fire toward the cellar. A muffled human yelp drifted upward through the boards, and the assault from the cellar ceased.

Now the gang members would think twice about attempting to come up through the hatch. Would they retreat into the yard?

"Help me tie up these guys," Sean called. "Then we can both turn our attention to holding off an attack."

Unintelligible squawks were coming from the sat phone she'd dropped. Hayley scooped up the handset and shushed her brother's near-hysterical questions.

"We're okay so far, but I've got to go," she said. "Just get here. Fast! And call in more help. Medics, too."

She ended the call and shrugged out of the pack weighing on her shoulders. Minor rummaging inside its contents produced rope suitable for binding their captives. Within minutes, she had both the weapons traffickers securely trussed up. Touching them sent her heart pounding and her skin crawling. Except for the man who shot her sister, Hayley had never been in close contact with anyone who literally wanted to kill her and would do so if given half a chance. For that reason, she tied them extra tight to the tune of curse words from the pilot, who had a lump growing on his forehead from the blow he'd received to subdue him. Patterson remained silent as she bound him, but his reptilian stare chilled her to the core.

"Good job." Sean gave her a nod. "Now we hang in there for twenty minutes."

A raucous laugh came from the man in the suit. "You don't have twenty minutes. My people will flank you on every side and rush in here."

Hayley's breath snagged, and her gaze darted toward Sean.

The ATF agent snorted. "I doubt that very much. They know we have you."

"But they also know I'm not a proper hostage." The kingpin thug sneered. "A fed can't threaten to kill me if my boys attack."

"He won't, but I might." The words growled from Hayley's throat, and she lifted her rifle to point directly at him. "You're the kind that will kill anyone, anywhere, for any reason or no reason."

Just like the vile creature who murdered her twin sister. The pulse throbbed in her neck, and blackness edged her vision. The suited man's wide gaze locked with hers, and his face washed pale. Hayley's finger tightened on the trigger.

"Hayley." Scarcely daring to breathe, Sean spoke her name softly and eased a step toward her.

She paid him no attention, her focus wholly on the man who had engineered the mortal danger invading her life. Anguish, fury and grief etched the planes of her lovely face. The human instinct for revenge had to be roaring through her, demanding retaliation in kind—not only for Patterson's current savage injustice, but also the cold-blooded murder of her sister by the same type of man. Yet Hayley stood frozen, able to put that final millimeter of pressure on the trigger but not doing so.

"Hayley," Sean gently said again.

Silent seconds ticked past. Gradually, tension ebbed from her frame and she lowered the rifle. Not all the way, but far enough.

Out of the corner of his eye, Sean caught Patterson's stiff figure suddenly sagging as if his muscles had turned to mush. Justice was surely served in the man tasting the sort of terror he callously inflicted on others. Further justice would have to wait for the court to decide.

Hayley's wide-eyed gaze met Sean's. "A part of me wanted to do it…but I couldn't."

"I know." Sean offered a tender smile and allowed himself a full breath. "He *would* snuff either of us out without a second thought, but that's not how you are. It's all about the difference between his depravity and your decency."

"Thank you." Her words were a whisper, and she turned her head away from him, blinking rapidly.

"We need to prepare for an assault," he said briskly. "First, we've got to verify that all windows and doors are secure."

"You'd better do it fast." Patterson's overly cocky tone smacked of bravado in compensation for his show of fear a few moments ago. "The gang will be coming after me pronto."

Sean narrowed his gaze on the man. "I'm not sure any of them like you well enough to risk their lives rescuing you. They just want to ensure Hayley and I aren't available to testify against them in court."

Patterson returned his glare. "I share that objective, and I don't give two hoots what any of those half-witted goons think of me as long as they do what I say. I don't run a fraternity—I run a business."

"You run a gang of low-life crooks." Hayley sniffed. "And you're the lowest of them all. Any other assessment is delusional."

Sean chuckled. "What she said."

She turned away and headed for the stairs. "I'm going to check the upstairs windows, Sean. Why don't you take a peek in the bathroom and make sure that window is barricaded the way they've done to the windows and doors on this bottom level?"

"I'll keep an eye on that kitchen floor hatch, too."

With one foot on the bottom step, Hayley turned toward him with a frown. "We have a lot of directions to keep an eye on."

Patterson chortled. "Too many for two people. We'll get you yet. The quiet out there isn't going to last many more seconds."

Heat erupted in Sean's gut. "You aren't going to think it's so funny when you find out how I intend to cut off access to the front of the cabin."

"One of your clever plans?" Hayley started up the stairs. "I like it."

"You don't know what it is yet," Sean called after her as she disappeared onto the upper level with Mack at her heels.

"No matter," she called back. "I already know I'll like it."

Sean's heart expanded. He'd never encountered unconditional approval before. At least, not for a long, long time. His plan had better prove worthy of her trust.

He quickly checked the bathroom window and discovered the crooks had nailed boards across it, too, as they'd done with the kitchen window. Now that Hayley and he were in possession of the cabin, the defensive measures were flipped to their benefit.

Sean returned his attention to their captives. The pilot he'd knocked on the noggin seemed content to huddle sullenly against the wall and not say a word. Patterson still knelt with a sneer cemented into his face. Sean grabbed the roller-wheeled desk chair and rumbled it across the floor to the gang leader.

"Sit." He pointed to the chair.

Huffing, the man staggered upright and settled onto the seat, spine rigid, staring straight ahead. Sean grabbed another length of rope and tied the gang leader's feet to the horizontal crosspieces above the rollers.

"You're taking me for a ride somewhere?" Patterson snarled. "I get it. You're going to perch me atop the hatch in the kitchen floor."

"That's a thought, but not the one I had in mind."

Sean hauled the chair backward toward the front door. He halted near a gun aperture carved into the plywood over the picture window.

"Trooper Glenn, are you out there?" he hollered.

"Don't you go talking to the turncoat cop, you undercover fed," Wade Becker's harsh tones responded from somewhere out of sight in the trees. "The only reason we were following the dirty cop is 'cause he knows his way around the bush. I'm in charge out here. Make no mistake."

"You might want to ask Patterson about who's in charge."

"As long as I get him out of there in one piece and shut you two up, I'll be in his good graces. You ready to surrender yet? We've got you outgunned, and we're about to come in blazing."

"You might want to rethink that idea. I'm about to open the front door and perch your boss on the threshold. If you try to shoot up the front of the cabin, you'll take him out."

Silence fell as Patterson's jaw dropped, and he began squirming against his bonds.

Sean grinned at him. "I see you're not entirely convinced your faithful minions will hold their fire for your sake."

He yanked open the front door and rolled Patterson's chair into the opening. No shots answered the movement. Sean released the breath he hadn't known he was holding. He really didn't want anyone to die on his watch, but if the ploy with the gang boss meant Hayley and he survived, it was a necessary risk.

"As you can see," he called out to their adversaries, "I'm a man who means what he says. I'm telling you now, help is on the way for Hayley and me. Already en route from Fairbanks. Less than twenty minutes out."

"You're lying!" Wade snarled.

"Nope. It's happening. So, we can all just hang around at a nice little impasse until they show up, or you might want to consider slinking off into the wilderness and trying to hide. I promise you the hunt is going to go the other way around soon enough."

"Don't listen to this guy!" Patterson roared. "It's only two people coming in a good plane. We can take the aircraft and—"

Hayley's figure darted past Sean and wrapped something around Patterson's mouth. It was her neck scarf. Then she skittered away from the open door, eyes wide, face pale.

"We can't let them overpower my brother and the trooper with him."

"We won't."

She blinked at him as if she wasn't sure whether to believe his assurance. The woman was nothing if not a realist. No one could make anyone else an absolute promise of safety, but he was going to do his utmost to make sure she didn't lose a brother, too, on top of losing her sister—much less their own lives.

"I'm going to call Craig again." She turned away and picked up the phone.

The conversation was brief with her brother, affirming they were less than ten minutes away.

"If the crew out there are going to try anything," Sean said, "it will be soon."

"I'll go upstairs and keep a lookout from those windows. Mack can watch the kitchen trap. He'll alert if anyone attempts that entrance again." She gave a terse command, and the malamute took up a post with his eyes on the kitchen.

Taut silence fell. Minutes ticked past as Sean stood to one side of the open front door, gaze scanning the area. The cold breeze penetrated the cabin, battling the heat of the blaze in the fireplace. Then the distant buzz of a plane engine broke through the stillness.

Sean's heart leaped, and he readied his weapon to fire. Patterson had suggested his guys attempt to take the plane. Hayley and he had to make sure that didn't happen.

An airplane with the Alaska State Trooper insignia swooped low over the property, then began to circle around. Sean divided his attention between glances at the plane, attention toward his prisoners and the tree line where potential attackers hid.

"Attention below," a voice blasted from a bullhorn above. "Surrender now, and you will be taken into custody unharmed. If you resist, be advised a helicopter carrying a SWAT team is on the way."

Sean nodded to himself. Smart. The trooper didn't plan to land until the suspects had shown themselves. Yet it was anyone's guess if that would happen. Wade was a knuckle-headed bully, but bullies were usually cowards.

"Lay down your weapons and show yourselves with your hands over your heads." The bullhorn voice spoke again as the plane performed another lazy circle overhead.

Movement came from the forest, and Sean tensed, ready to answer an attack. Figures trickled out of the woods, arms raised, except for one thug who stumbled forth with his arm in a sling. No doubt, the one Mack had savaged. That guy was probably feeling a whole lot worse than Sean with his bullet crease.

Next to him, Patterson was wriggling in his chair, spewing something unintelligible from his mouth against the gag. Cussing a blue streak, no doubt. The man was done for, along with his gang of weapons smugglers. A great weariness filtered through Sean, but he shook off the draining sensation. He had to stay alert until the last man was cuffed.

"I'll keep my weapon trained on these guys out there until you've got them subdued," Hayley called from overhead.

"Sounds good," he called back. "I'll leave Mack in charge of Patterson and his pilot."

He grabbed more rope and headed out into the cold. While he bound the glaring, snarling thugs, the trooper plane came in for a landing and skidded up onto the beach. From the passenger side, a tall, slender man with dark hair emerged, bearing a rifle over a crooked elbow, and strode toward the cabin. From the pilot seat, a husky, middle-aged man climbed out and approached Sean's location at a trot, one hand on the gun butt protruding from his hip holster.

Sean gaped at the second man. "Uncle Tate?" That was right. His mother's brother had been a state trooper. Did the guy recognize him? "It's me. Your nephew Sean."

Tate halted several feet away and regarded him soberly. "Is it really Adele's boy?"

Sean's insides curdled. If his father was to be believed, his mother's people didn't want to have anything to do with him.

He squared his shoulders. "Sean O'Keefe in the flesh. I'm an ATF agent now."

A tentative smile grew on his uncle's face. "It's good to see you." He extended a beefy paw.

"Really?" Sean took the man's calloused hand.

"You've been a stranger too long."

Warmth spread through Sean's insides as he met his uncle's friendly gaze. He'd have to explore the meaning of this unexpected welcome after he put the necessary call in to his ATF handler.

"Where's Hayley?" a voice cried out, jerking Sean out of mentally preparing his report to his superiors.

He looked around to find Hayley's lanky brother running toward them.

"She's in the cabin," Sean answered.

"There's no one in there except Mack and some guy with a bump on his head tied up on the floor."

Sean gazed around at the smuggling crew subdued at his feet, and an anomaly hit him. Traitor Trooper Glenn wasn't among them.

Mack's throaty bark rang out from the rear of the property near the lake, but it was the roar of an airplane engine from that vicinity that yanked Sean's head in that direction. The sound wasn't coming from the plane that had just arrived. That aircraft stood in clear sight. No, someone was trying to escape in the plane he'd damaged with gunfire yesterday. Evidently, the aircraft wasn't unmanageably crippled.

Heart in his throat, Sean ran toward the lake and as he swept past the cabin, the plane came into sight. It was already taxiing across the water for takeoff. Three heads were visible. Patterson in a rear passenger seat. Glenn in the pilot seat. And in the copilot's position sat Hayley.

She was a hostage on the plane with Patterson pointing a gun at her head.

# FIFTEEN

Hayley squeezed her hands into white-knuckled fists, suppressing the inward quaking that was slowly turning her insides to jelly. They'd been so close to being rescued. How had she ended up in the clutches of murderous crooks, flying with them away from capture in a plane that Sean had put bullets into and might not be airworthy?

Simple answer. She'd let her guard down when the crew outside emerged from the forest to surrender. She hadn't thought to make sure Glenn was among the subdued crooks. Her brother's false friend had sneaked into the cabin through the cellar. Mack hadn't alerted because he knew Glenn, and the man's entrance didn't raise his hackles.

While Sean was outside helping secure the prisoners, the treacherous trooper had gotten the drop on her with his automatic weapon and taken her hostage. He ordered her to free his boss and now, without any kind of pre-flight checks, the airplane's skids were leaving the lake. They were headed off to who knew where.

"Where are you taking us, Glenn?" Patterson demanded as if he'd overheard Hayley's thoughts. "We're going to be under hot pursuit almost immediately."

"I've got a cousin who owns a homestead near Nenana. He'll hide us and help us escape."

"That's almost a hundred miles from here," Hayley said. "Will this shot-up wreck make it that far, or are we going to end up emergency landing in the wilderness?"

The plane's engine stuttered, punctuating her question, but then it caught and hummed steadily again. Patterson jabbed the barrel of his gun into her seat back, jolting her.

"No one asked for your input, woman," the crime boss snarled. "My pilot taped up the hole in the punctured hose as soon as we got back to your homestead yesterday."

*Great!* They were flying into the middle of nowhere, in an aircraft held together by duct tape applied by the pilot his boss had callously abandoned in her cabin.

Hayley looked over her shoulder out the window. They were almost out of sight of her homestead, and the forest was skimming past beneath them. Sean had to be ripping his hair out at the escape of the crime boss he was after. Surely, having a fit on her account, as well. Patterson was right in thinking someone would be coming after them pronto.

But once this plane was out of sight, how easy would it be for anyone to find them? And even if someone did, what could they do when she was in the bad guys' clutches as a hostage?

Throughout this whole ordeal, she hadn't felt anything like despair, but now the darkness clutched her close. As soon as she was no longer essential to their freedom and survival, these people would kill her without batting an eyelash. She touched her mouth with the tips of her fingers. Sean had kissed her, and she had kissed him back. A foolish, fleeting moment? Or the promise of something true and beautiful to come? Now, she might never have the chance to find out.

As the escaping plane gained altitude away from the homestead, Sean whirled on his heels and raced back to his uncle standing guard over the prisoners. Hayley's brother was circling the cabin, calling Hayley's name. Apparently, he hadn't seen her in the cockpit of the aircraft that took off.

"We need to confine these guys in the cellar of the cabin," he told his uncle Tate. "Either you or Craig can stand guard over them until the helicopter arrives. Someone's got to fly me after the escapees. They've got Hayley."

"What?" Hayley's brother cried out as he jogged toward them. "I'm a pilot. Let's go."

Tate lifted a forestalling hand. "That's a state trooper plane, son. I'll have to fly it. Can you watch these bozos until SWAT gets here?"

Hayley's brother shifted from foot to foot, darting glances toward the empty sky. "Sure, sure. Just get going, would you? I *can't* lose this sister, too."

Sean put a hand on the man's shoulder. "I'll do everything I can to get her back. I care about her, too."

Craig's eyebrows lifted as his dark eyes bored into Sean's, but he made no comment on the declaration.

The three of them shooed the prisoners down the steps into the dark cellar and secured the outdoor entrance with the same board that had been there before. Craig went inside with Mack to stand guard over the kitchen hatch. Not that any of the thugs would be well-advised to attempt climbing out that way with their hands bound and a dog ready to pounce.

Minutes later, Sean and Tate were in the air, heading away from the homestead in the direction the plane carrying Hayley had gone. There was no sign of that aircraft in any direction.

"How are we going to find them?" Sean asked his uncle. "There's so much wilderness out here."

"That's a short-range plane so they'll need to find some semblance of civilization and another mode of transportation relatively quickly. Nenana's the nearest town, and Trooper Cauley's got a few relatives in that area."

"You know Glenn?" Sean shot his stoic-faced uncle a sharp glance.

"Cops are a special community to themselves, particularly troopers out here. I've been on missions with him before. He *was* a stand-up guy." The man shook his head. "How he went dirty I'll never understand."

Sean snorted. "Money talks and Sherman Patterson speaks that language fluently and persuasively."

"Let me report our status to the station."

Sean sat quietly, straining his gaze in every direction for a glimpse of their quarry. The sky remained maddeningly clear blue. Not a speck anywhere on the horizon.

His uncle updated the station dispatcher, leaving instructions to notify the en-route SWAT team of the situation and to be on the lookout for Trooper Cauley's aircraft.

"Are you able to pick up the tracking signal from his plane?" Tate added.

Sean's heart leaped. Could locating the fleeing criminals and their precious cargo be so easy?"

The dispatcher responded in the negative. "He must have disabled it."

Sean's heart flopped to his toes. Locating the fugitives and, more importantly, Hayley, just got exponentially more difficult.

Hayley gripped the edges of her seat as the engine started spluttering again only thirty minutes into the flight. Her stomach knotted. This was it. They were going down.

Judging by Glenn's muttered curse words,

he knew it, too. He fiddled with the instrumentation and fought the yoke to keep the plane aloft, but it was a losing battle. The engine's coughs died into a long, high whine, and then they were gliding steadily toward earth.

"Get that engine started and get us out of here." Patterson's snarl broke the silence that had fallen upon the loss of engine noise.

Glenn audibly gulped. "I'm sorry, sir. Whatever fix was made on this plane, it didn't hold."

"I'm not going trekking through this wilderness, so figure something out."

Heat boiled up in Hayley's gut. She twisted in her seat and glared at the gang leader. "Shut your mouth. We're landing whether you like it or not. Unless you'd rather crash than glide in, you'd better let the pilot concentrate."

The body of the aircraft began to quake, and Patterson's face washed white. He scowled and brandished his weapon at her but subsided into silence.

Hayley looked toward Glenn. Beads of sweat had popped out on the man's forehead.

He darted her a sidelong glance. "Help me find a clearing where we can land."

Her gaze searched the terrain. They were skimming over thick forestation, and gravity was steadily pulling them, willy-nilly, toward the sharp evergreen spires. But any attempt to put down among the trees would be catastrophic for the aircraft and everyone aboard. Hayley's skin crawled.

"There!" she cried out. "A patch of marsh."

Glenn let out a grunt and swiftly adjusted course.

The wet terrain would be compatible with the landing skids on the amphibious aircraft, but the open area was smaller than Hayley wanted to see. However, they had no time to look for a better landing spot. The treetops were rushing toward them at an alarming rate.

Hayley tightened her seat belt. The breath froze in her lungs as they neared the open patch.

Almost there.

They might make it.

The nose of the plane thrust beyond the trees, but branches snagged the tail, slowing momentum and wrenching the craft into a downward dip. Glenn battled the controls, frantically attempting to level the wings and raise the nose, but the ground was too close and the plane was too slow to respond.

Screams erupted from every throat as they plunged toward the earth.

* * *

Sean used his uncle's radio to call in a terse status report to his ATF handler. He could care less about the huge *attaboy* he received from her for successfully sabotaging the sale of the drone. All he cared about was retrieving Hayley safe and sound.

His handler promised to check into current satellite coverage on his location to see if one could spot the rogue aircraft. For that, Sean awarded her a heartfelt thank-you. The lack of cloud cover would make eyes in the sky possible, though it was anyone's guess if a satellite was anywhere in the vicinity.

He'd scarcely spoken to God since the death of his mother, but at this moment, he broke away from his aggrieved silent treatment toward the Almighty and inaudibly poured his heart out. He didn't try to bargain. His mom had taught him dealmaking wasn't the way things worked with God. Every blessing came by grace alone. Adele O'Keefe had been vibrant in her faith, which was why Sean never could understand why she died so young and left him behind. Maybe it was time to stop demanding explanations and throw himself on God's mercy.

In the background of his prayers, Sean

registered his uncle engaging in a series of radio contacts with various authorities, including the park rangers at Denali State Park located in the opposite direction from Hayley's homestead. Park service planes would join the search in case Trooper Cauley had doubled back and headed in that direction instead of shooting for Nenana. Other aircrafts in a two-hundred mile radius were taking to the air to join the hunt, though civilians were warned to keep their distance and only report nysightings.

"You have a lot of contacts," Sean said to Tate.

The man awarded him a lopsided grin. "Folks out here look out for each other."

"I remember that. I remember…a lot of things."

The conversation flagged for several minutes as their gazes swept the horizon for any sign of their quarry. Then Tate's head swiveled in Sean's direction. The man's expression was dark. Sean would even call it hurt.

"A big hole was left in our family when your mom died," he said, "and you and your dad suddenly moved away."

"I lived in that hole for a lot of years."

Tate nodded and pursed his lips. "Your

dad probably thought he was doing the right thing."

"Did he? I don't know. He never talked to me about his reasons other than to hint we were no longer welcome with my mom's people. I thought the estrangement was my fault."

Tate let out a soft growl.

"Not true?" Sean narrowed his gaze on his uncle.

The man shook his head. "Not at all. When tragedy strikes, family should pull together. But your father hated living in the Interior."

Sean barked a laugh. "He never did like anywhere away from the ocean. The two of us need to have a long conversation the next time I see him."

"After that, maybe you could visit us here in the bush."

"No maybe about it. I'll do it."

Uncle Tate grinned but sobered quickly. "Let's find this girl of yours and arrest some bad guys."

The fist around Sean's heart tightened its grip. *Hayley, where are you?*

A sudden brightness to the north and east of them grabbed his attention. Fire? A plane crash? His insides twisted. No, that was a flare. Someone was signaling distress.

"There!" Sean pointed.

"I see it," Tate said and adjusted their flight path.

Tense seconds ticked past as Sean strained his eyes to see what might lie below. A lost or injured hunter with nothing to do with their search? Or maybe one of the searchers in trouble? A downed aircraft? Possibly even the one they sought. How did he dare hope when there was a possibility he hoped in vain? Then again, how could he not hope? Hope was all he had.

*Yes!* He recognized the crumpled state trooper aircraft lying on the marshy ground below.

*Nooo!* The wreckage was a twisted mess. How had anyone survived? More to the point, *who* had survived to send up the flare?

Then a slender figure standing away from the wreckage caught his eye. The person was frantically waving up at them. No other life showed itself below.

Uncle Tate brought his aircraft around in a circle, then headed toward the ground. The landing was tight, but the man pulled it off as smoothly as if they had ample space.

The second the plane stopped, Sean leaped out the door and raced toward the one who had sent up the flare. His boots splashed marsh water onto his jeans, chilling his legs, but he paid no attention. Out of the corner of his eye, he dimly registered his uncle approaching the downed aircraft with his service pistol drawn. No signs of life emanated from the crashed plane, but if anyone else had survived, Tate had the threat handled.

Sean spread out his arms and caught Hayley as she crumpled against him.

"I've got you now," he murmured into her ear. "And I'm never leaving you."

# SIXTEEN

Huddled in one of the passenger seats of Trooper Tate's plane, Hayley drew the blanket Sean had given her close about her shoulders. Sean and his uncle were investigating the remains of Glenn Cauley's twisted aircraft. Hayley shivered—but not from cold—as she relived the crash.

The screams.

The acrid odor of sweat-soaked fear.

The screech of twisting metal.

The wrenching jolt of a fragile flying machine meeting solid earth.

The crash of shattering glass.

Blinding pain.

Then nothing.

Hayley touched her forehead where a fresh bandage covered a cut and a swollen lump. How long she'd been unconscious she could only guess. Probably only a short time because the sun had only moved marginally through the sky when she groggily regained consciousness to find warm blood seeping down her cheek and into one eye. Clearing her vision with the back of her hand, she'd found herself seated at a sideways angle, her seat belt holding her fast. The plane had landed hard on the pilot's side, snapping the wing and then skidding a significant distance. Her own side of the aircraft was relatively free from damage.

She'd looked toward Glenn. His body was contorted at an odd angle. Broken bones for sure. He was unconscious, breathing but not spurting blood anywhere. Then she'd looked toward Patterson. The man was groaning woozily, but he didn't open his eyes. Immediately, Hayley had snatched the gun from him, then helped herself to Glenn's automatic and his sidearm. Whatever else the crooks did, they couldn't shoot her now.

Upon assuring herself a margin of safety, summoning help became the top priority. She tried the radio, but it didn't work. Just as despair gripped her heart, she'd remembered the flare gun. Standard equipment. With frantic, shaking hands, she'd found it, then half stumbled, half fell out of the aircraft onto the marshy ground. It had taken all her strength in a body wracked with painful bruises and cuts, but she'd managed to pull the trigger. The flare ascended, but a question remained in her mind: Would anyone see it?

As if in answer to a prayer she hadn't had the presence of mind to utter, Sean did see it. His uncle's plane landed, and he ran to her, held her and spoke words of promise in her ear. Did he mean it when he said he wouldn't leave?

Her gaze fastened on his efficient movements at the downed plane. At last, he backed out of the passenger door, stepped to the ground and turned toward her. With long strides, he approached where she sat, opened the door and climbed in beside her.

"How are you doing?" he asked, his dark gaze searching hers.

"Still processing," she managed to mumble.

"Are you hurting anywhere particular?"

"Just everywhere." She attempted a laugh, but her muscles spasmed at the effort and the noise turned into a whimper. "I think my body is one giant bruise."

Sean's hand wrapped around one of hers. "A helicopter is on the way to transport you and the suspects to the hospital."

"How are those two?" She jerked her chin toward the wreckage.

Sean afforded her a taut grin. "Patterson seems to be the same giant bruise you are, but he's spitting mad at being caught. Cauley's in a bad way. I don't know if he'll make it."

Hayley turned her head and gazed out across the starkly beautiful wilderness. "My brother's going to be doubly devastated if Glenn doesn't pull through. They were friends from boyhood. Death on top of betrayal would be like losing him twice."

"Would you like to talk to him?"

"Who?"

"Your brother."

"Please."

Sean snatched up the radio handset, gave it to her and then put the call through. Moments later, her brother's familiar tones touched her ears. Unable to help herself, Hayley burst into tears. Dimly, Hayley registered Sean exiting the plane and leaving her to an emotional outpouring to her brother of all that had happened.

Soon enough, the *whump-whump* of helicopter noise drew close.

"I've got to go," she told Craig.

"Yes, definitely get somewhere for medical attention," he answered. "There's a SWAT team here at the homestead taking the rest of these creeps into custody. I'll hitch a ride with SWAT and see you at the hospital in Fairbanks as soon as I can make it."

Hayley ended the transmission, and within minutes, was escorted to the rescue helicopter. While a medic assessed her, a shackled, bedraggled Patterson was ushered into a seat behind and to one side of her in the large chopper. An armed guard took a seat beside him.

Sean stuck his head in the door and glared at the man. "Not one word to Hayley. Do you hear me?" He shook his finger at the smuggler.

Patterson scowled and stared toward his feet.

Sean turned toward her, his gaze softening. "This lowlife won't be bothering you anymore."

She sent him a tentative smile. He was looking after her, but did such gallantry mean anything beyond the courtesy he would afford any crime victim? Maybe. After all, as soon as his uncle's aircraft touched down, he ran to *her*, not toward the crashed plane to secure his nemesis, Patterson. He'd put her first. Her heart tripped faster.

What was the matter with her? She wasn't supposed to fall for another law enforcement type. Yet here she was, hoping with everything in her that the end of the danger didn't also mean the end of the relationship. Did he also hope the same?

A stretcher bearing Glenn's still figure was brought into the rear compartment, EMTs clambered aboard and the chopper's engine fired up. A dull weight dropped into Hayley's stomach. Wasn't Sean riding with her? Probably too much to expect when he had the opportunity to fly to Fairbanks with his uncle and get reacquainted with him. That circumstance could possibly reconcile him with his entire maternal family.

Hayley chewed her lower lip. Looking at the situation in that light, she could hardly blame Sean for his choice. She leaned her head back against the rest and closed her eyes, anticipating liftoff at any moment.

The side door suddenly flung open, sending a surge of chilly air into the cabin. Hayley's eyes popped wide to behold Sean boarding the helicopter with only a slight wince to indicate lingering pain from his bullet wound and broken rib. His smile and the warmth of his gaze took her breath away as he strapped himself into the seat beside her.

"What about your uncle?" she asked.

"What about him?"

"I thought you would want to be with him. Take the opportunity to do the whole reconciliation thing, you know."

Sean nodded. "Oh, that's going to happen. No problem. I've got a standing invitation."

"I'm glad." She beamed a smile at him, then winced at a sudden stab of pain in her head.

"Relax now, sweetheart. You're safe. We're both safe." He tenderly fitted a set of noise-canceling protectors over her ears, and the engine roar muted as the helicopter left the ground.

*Sweetheart. He called me sweetheart.*

The tension ebbed from her body as her head rested against his sturdy shoulder. Warm oblivion took her.

In a blink, the jolt of landing on the hospital helipad awakened her. Things began to happen quickly, and soon medical staff were administering neurological and cognitive testing. Finally, after a CT scan of her skull, she found herself tucked away in a hospital bed.

Sean sat at her side and held her hand. Life had gone from terrifying and dangerous to pretty much perfect. *If I were a cat*, she mused as consciousness faded, *I would be purring*.

When she awakened, Sean was gone and her brother had taken the man's place at her bedside. Craig rose and leaned over her as she blinked her eyes to regain focus.

"How are you feeling?" he asked.

"Like I was in a plane wreck. But I'm alive, and that's huge." She smiled up at the familiar face. "Sorry for interrupting your writing research with my little crisis."

"*Little* crisis?" Craig snorted. "Understatement of the year. Agent O'Keefe filled in some of the blanks for me."

Hayley's gaze swept the room. "Where *is* Sean?"

"He had to go. Something about an official debriefing and doing a mountain of paperwork."

"Did he say when he's coming back?"

"Why would he come back?" Craig's brow furrowed.

Hayley opened her mouth, then closed it with a snap. Too soon to let Craig in on any budding romantic feelings between Sean and her. Not when uncertainties plagued her mind. Sean not leaving with Craig a message of intent to return left a sour taste in Hayley's mouth.

She wriggled herself into a more comfortable position in the bed. "He's got relatives in the Fairbanks area that he hasn't seen in a while. I thought maybe he'd want to visit with them."

"Oh. I guess I don't know anything about that. Only one thing I care about, and that's getting you home and comfortable in our winter digs here in Fairbanks."

Hayley shook her head. "Home to the homestead. I have a carving to finish and ship."

Craig's eyes widened. "You intend to complete the project yet this fall? Today is the first of October. The snow will close in to stay very soon."

"I gave my word to the buyer. Besides, we need to get the cabin windows repaired before winter sets in."

Her brother heaved a sigh. "You got me there."

"How's Mack?"

Craig grinned. "Healthy and missing you."

A knock sounded at the door, and Hayley's pulse jumped. Had Sean returned? A short, plump man in a medical jacket stepped into the room, and her heart sank. Not Sean. Was he doing the debriefing and paperwork here in Fairbanks, or had he needed to return to Anchorage? How maddening not to know. She didn't even have his cell phone number to call him, nor did he have hers.

Hayley firmed her jaw. If Sean O'Keefe wanted to see her again, he would have to seek her out. He knew where she lived. Until then, she would do her best not to get her hopes up. Too bad her best might not be good enough.

One week later, Hayley stood in her studio, putting the finishing touches on the thick and bulky packaging around the fish and eagle carving. Normally, when the time came to ship a project to the new owner, she'd be bubbling over with a mix of nerves—would they like the finished product?—and excitement— always thrilling to complete a piece!—but this time, she could summon neither trepidation nor triumph. Completing this carving, which she had thought was to be her magnum opus, filled no void in her heart.

Her emotional repertoire had shrunk to a dull, scarcely tolerable ache in the middle of her chest. Had she truly expected Sean to care about remaining in her life now that he must be the man of the hour with the ATF? He was probably receiving accolades and a promotion with his bureau, possibly even with the perk of choosing his station anywhere in the country.

Hayley patted the wrapped carving. At least, the buyer hadn't been upset when she'd had to call and notify him of a few bullet holes in the piece. She'd offered to reduce the price, but he wouldn't hear of it. In fact, he'd seemed a bit thrilled at the unique opportunity for bragging rights on owning a carving with such a tale of adventure attached to it.

Outside, Mack's throaty bark erupted. Hayley went to the door and peered outside. Nothing unusual in view. The landscape had lost significant color after the first deep frost and snowfall endured by Sean and her in the wilderness. The vegetation lay brown and dead, the roots waiting until spring for new shoots to spring up.

Mack continued barking, his nose poked toward the sky. A shiver traced a chilly finger down her spine at the déjà vu of the last time she'd stood in her shop doorway gazing at her dog while he alerted her to the approach of an aircraft. Hayley tamped down the negative reaction. This time, she was expecting a transport plane.

Hayley shrugged on her warm parka and stepped outside into the cold with her gaze focused skyward. Sure enough, a large-bellied airplane popped into view over the treetops and dipped for a landing in her lake. The craft splashed down and rumbled to the fire-damaged dock. Hayley loped forward to help the pilot and crew tie off, but before her boots reached the first dock board, a tall figure leaped from the passenger side. She practically skidded to a halt, her jaw falling open.

Grinning from ear to ear, the man strode toward her and halted within arm's reach. Those familiar dark eyes searched her face. The grin faded but warmth remained.

"You're every bit as beautiful as I remember."

Sean's words caressed Hayley's heart. Heat flushed through her cheeks, and a laugh bubbled from her throat.

"Oh, please," she said. "I have packing material in my hair."

"Yes." He plucked a bit of something from beside her ear. "But your accessories are uniquely you."

"You're here. I can hardly believe it."

"Why?" He tilted his head. "I told you I'd be out of touch, but I'd be back as soon as I wrapped things up at headquarters."

"When did you tell me that?"

"In the hospital before I left."

"I don't remember that conversation. I only remember waking up to find you gone and my brother there."

Sean let out a low groan and kneaded his forehead with his fingertips. "My bad! I should have made sure you were truly awake when I spoke to you. But you did answer me, so I thought—"

Hayley touched his arm. "It's okay. How were you to know I wouldn't remember the conversation? Those painkillers really knocked me for a loop."

"So, you've been wondering about me all this time?" His shoulders slumped. "Or maybe you forgot about me. Do you want me with you?" He spoke the question like every word weighed a ton.

She dropped her gaze and let out a long breath, then lifted her eyes to his. "I do want you with me, but what about your career? There's no ATF office in Fairbanks or any-where nearby. I have no interest in moving to Anchorage, and I'm not sure a long-distance relationship would work. I—"

Warm lips on hers stifled her words. Sean gathered her into a close embrace. Her arms lifted and wrapped around his neck, returning the kiss with everything in her. If this was the last kiss they shared, she wanted the memory to warm her heart forever. At last, Sean lifted his head but didn't release her from his arms.

"I like it here in the Alaskan bush. The same way the ocean feels like home to my dad; this feels like home to me. I finished the debriefing and reports with the ATF and turned in my resignation. I even had a long, air-clearing conversation with my father. Now, I've got my application in with the Alaska State Troopers, and Uncle Tate assures me I'm a lock for the job. They're short a trooper, you know. But the most important piece is you." He dropped his arms away from her and stepped back. "I'm falling in love with you, Hayley Brent. Do you want to see where this relationship might go?"

Hayley began to nod like her head was on a spring. "I'm falling in love with you, Sean O'Keefe. I didn't want to at first, but I am, and I'm glad. I thank God for you dropping in uninvited, even if you brought a crew of crooks with you. I'd even thank *them* for the privilege of meeting you if I wouldn't rather slap them instead."

Sean laughed and opened his arms to her.

She leaped into them so hard they both staggered. Mack pranced around them, tail wagging like a banner as Sean and she stood together, laughing and kissing, and kissing and laughing.

The breakthrough in Hayley's life was not a carved eagle, but this man God sent her under the wildest circumstances imaginable. They had survived by learning to trust each other and renewing their trust in God. With Him in the middle of their relationship, old griefs would heal, and Sean and she would complete each other in a full life worth living.

\* \* \* \* \*

Dear Reader,

Thank you for joining Hayley and Sean in their wild outdoor adventure. I hope you enjoyed meeting Mack, too. He's a gutsy, sassy one. What a pleasure it's been to write about them and share their story with you.

Not many of us will ever find ourselves in a situation like Hayley and Sean, being hunted through the wilderness by crooks bent on killing them, but few of us have led lives unscathed by loss or trauma. Many of us, like Sean, struggle to cope with our feelings of guilt for foolish or even silly small things we've done or not done that seem connected to larger tragedies. Or, as in Hayley's case, we find ourselves years later still living in unhealthy ways or with unhealthy attitudes because of a senseless tragedy in our pasts.

Whatever the case for you, my prayer is that Sean and Hayley's story provide some glimmer of a way forward in living out your own stories. As Sean and Hayley discovered, an honest look at themselves, a conversation with a trusted other who regards them with a nonjudgmental eye and a simple but profound change of perspective can begin to mend the broken places. May truth bathed in grace and hope set you free.

I enjoy hearing from my readers. My email address is jnelson@jillelizabethnelson.com. You can also communicate with me through my website, jillelizabethnelson.com. Or you can reach me at www.Facebook.com/jillelizabethnelson.author.

Abundant blessings,
*Jill*

# Get 4 FREE REWARDS!

## We'll send you 2 FREE Books plus 2 FREE Mystery Gifts.

FREE
Value Over
$20

Both the **Love Inspired®** and **Love Inspired®** Suspense series feature compelling novels filled with inspirational romance, faith, forgiveness, and hope.

---

**YES!** Please send me 2 FREE novels from the Love Inspired or Love Inspired Suspense series and my 2 FREE gifts (gifts are worth about $10 retail). After receiving them, if I don't wish to receive any more books, I can return the shipping statement marked "cancel." If I don't cancel, I will receive 6 brand-new Love Inspired Larger-Print books or Love Inspired Suspense Larger-Print books every month and be billed just $6.24 each in the U.S. or $6.49 each in Canada. That is a savings of at least 17% off the cover price. It's quite a bargain! Shipping and handling is just 50¢ per book in the U.S. and $1.25 per book in Canada.* I understand that accepting the 2 free books and gifts places me under no obligation to buy anything. I can always return a shipment and cancel at any time by calling the number below. The free books and gifts are mine to keep no matter what I decide.

Choose one: ☐ **Love Inspired**
Larger-Print
(122/322 IDN GRDF)

☐ **Love Inspired Suspense**
Larger-Print
(107/307 IDN GRDF)

Name (please print)

Address                                                                                          Apt. #

City                                    State/Province                          Zip/Postal Code

**Email:** Please check this box ☐ if you would like to receive newsletters and promotional emails from Harlequin Enterprises ULC and its affiliates. You can unsubscribe anytime.

---

### Mail to the Harlequin Reader Service:
**IN U.S.A.:** P.O. Box 1341, Buffalo, NY 14240-8531
**IN CANADA:** P.O. Box 603, Fort Erie, Ontario L2A 5X3

**Want to try 2 free books from another series?** Call 1-800-873-8635 or visit www.ReaderService.com.

*Terms and prices subject to change without notice. Prices do not include sales taxes, which will be charged (if applicable) based on your state or country of residence. Canadian residents will be charged applicable taxes. Offer not valid in Quebec. This offer is limited to one order per household. Books received may not be as shown. Not valid for current subscribers to the Love Inspired or Love Inspired Suspense series. All orders subject to approval. Credit or debit balances in a customer's account(s) may be offset by any other outstanding balance owed by or to the customer. Please allow 4 to 6 weeks for delivery. Offer available while quantities last.

**Your Privacy**—Your information is being collected by Harlequin Enterprises ULC, operating as Harlequin Reader Service. For a complete summary of the information we collect, how we use this information and to whom it is disclosed, please visit our privacy notice located at corporate.harlequin.com/privacy-notice. From time to time we may also exchange your personal information with reputable third parties. If you wish to opt out of this sharing of your personal information, please visit readerservice.com/consumerschoice or call 1-800-873-8635. **Notice to California Residents**—Under California law, you have specific rights to control and access your data. For more information on these rights and how to exercise them, visit corporate.harlequin.com/california-privacy.

LIRLIS22R2

# THE 2022 LOVE INSPIRED CHRISTMAS COLLECTION

## Buy 3 and get 1 FREE!

**May all that is beautiful, meaningful and brings you joy be yours this holiday season...including this fun-filled collection featuring 24 Christmas stories. From tender holiday romances to Christmas Eve suspense, this collection has it all.**

YES! Please send me the **2022 LOVE INSPIRED CHRISTMAS COLLECTION** in Larger Print! This collection begins with ONE FREE book and 2 FREE gifts in the first shipment. Along with my FREE book, I'll get another 3 Larger Print books! If I do not cancel, I will continue to receive four books a month for five more months. Each shipment will contain another FREE gift. I'll pay just $23.97 U.S./$26.97 CAN., plus $1.99 U.S./$4.99 CAN. for shipping and handling per shipment.* I understand that accepting the free books and gifts places me under no obligation to buy anything. I can always return a shipment and cancel at any time. My free books and gifts are mine to keep no matter what I decide.

☐ 298 HCK 0958          ☐ 498 HCK 0958

Name (please print)

Address                                                    Apt. #

City                          State/Province              Zip/Postal Code

### Mail to the Harlequin Reader Service:
**IN U.S.A.: P.O. Box 1341, Buffalo, NY 14240-8531**
**IN CANADA: P.O. Box 603, Fort Erie, ON L2A 5X3**